A
Different
Spring

Maggie Redding

For June Mulgrew

In their shady corners of the garden, the snowdrops had appeared as though overnight. During the weeks after Christmas, Lydia always went out to look for them. There they were, this year, modest, low, a small promise of spring. She and Peter had first found them when they moved into the house nearly twenty-five years ago. For twenty of those years, she had ventured out into the cold with him, to the soggy garden, to find them, the last time when he was ill. They had linked arms to tread carefully from corner to corner, she supporting him. A few weeks later he died.

This afternoon, she was on her way to visit her daughters, neither of whom she had seen since Christmas. Both lived within walking distance of her home, a short bus ride if it was wet. And today it was wet, pouring with rain. Yes, they were busy, Kate and Ellie, with their own lives, she knew and accepted that. She missed them all the same, and her grandchildren. At the bus stop she hailed the first bus to appear. It was empty.

"Not many customers today," she said, as she presented her bus pass to the driver, a young, black woman.

"None at all, apart from you," the driver said. "Who can blame them, this weather? You must be going somewhere nice."

Lydia sat on the seat closest to the front of the bus. "Only to see my family," she said.

"Families!" the driver said with a laugh. "Who needs them?"

"I do," Lydia said. "I'm lonely without them."

"Aw, bless you. Live on your own, do you?" She was cheerful and warm. She drove slowly.

"Yes. Five years now. My husband died. I'd never lived alone."

"Must be hard for you."

"It is, at times. Especially now, after Christmas, and in this weather."

"Are you feeling a bit down in the dumps?"

"I hate to admit it, but I am, really."

"You know what I reckon? I reckon, if you feel down, don't fight it. Stay with it until it tires of you. Otherwise, it'll jump up and grab you when you're not looking." She laughed a happy laugh that belied her words.

"D'you know, I think that's what must have happened, I've resisted it. I'll remember that. You sound a bit disillusioned with your family."

"Some of them. Parents and grandparents and so forth. Not to mention certain aunts and uncles."

"Strife in families seems to be quite normal. It doesn't improve when you get older. It magnifies. It's the children and grandchildren too, then. Always treading on eggshells, I am."

"Eggshells, eh? I think my lot want me to walk on water!"

Lydia laughed. The young woman sounded so energetic, she was a tonic.

"Can I have Bertha Road, please?"

"So soon? I'll have no one to talk to if you go."

"You shouldn't be talking, really, should you? But I'm glad you did. What you said rang a bell. I'll remember it."

Lydia alighted. The driver gave a grin and waved as the bus moved off.

All smiles, Lydia waved back before moving on to the turning where Ellie lived.

Yes, it had grabbed her, this misery, this grieving, whatever it was. It had grabbed her by the throat and however hard she fought it, now she couldn't shake it off. Surely it was time? Five years. He would never have demanded that, expected that. It wasn't Peter's fault, was it, so it must be hers. It had been her choice, not to live fully, although she knew it wasn't what he would have wanted for her. "I'll be fine," he had said. "I'm going to a place with no cares. Remember that and get the best out of life."

But how to do that, she didn't really know.

Ellie, her youngest daughter, was busy. Lydia didn't even bother to knock on the door. The house was small, in a Victorian terrace, facing straight onto the pavement, built for railway workers. The curtains were drawn at the window of the front room downstairs, a sign that Ellie was probably immersed in yards of tulle or silk, measuring a young woman for a wedding dress. An accomplished seamstress, Ellie also did alterations and repairs, especially shortening trousers, or taking in too-large shirts for young, single men, providing many opportunities for meeting a prospective husband, or so Lydia thought.

Lydia set off for the home of her older daughter, Kate, less than ten minutes further on. The rain had eased a little and so had Lydia's mood. She should speak to strangers more often. That encounter with the bus driver had been a real uplift.

Kate, with husband Dan and children, Nick and

3

Polly, lived at forty-seven Alexandra Street, an Edwardian terraced house, the sort of house that stretched back one room at a time. Kate and Dan had been there since they married, eighteen years ago. This house was further from the town centre and was bigger than Ellie's.

Lydia surveyed it as she approached. The window-frames looked as if they could do with a coat of paint. From the front, the roof appeared to be intact, no slipped tiles, not even over the bay. The small front garden was neglected, but at this time of the year, looked little different from its neighbours. She pushed the gate open and closed it firmly behind her to hurry up the short, tiled pathway to the front door. She rang the bell. After a long wait, Kate opened the door a crack.

"Mum," she said, pulling the door wider.

"Hello, Kate."

"I didn't think it could be you just yet. I've only just got in from school. You're wet."

"No matter." Lydia stepped in. "How are you? I went to Ellie's first, but she had someone there." She hung her wet coat on a peg in the hall, letting it drip onto the tiled floor. "I walked as slowly as I could because I knew I'd be early."

"She gets busy as this time of the year, between Christmas and Easter. Tea, Mum?"

"Don't make it specially."

"I'm making it anyway. Go on in." Kate ushered her mother into the sitting room. "Polly's not home yet."

Kate left to go to the kitchen. Lydia sank awkwardly into a chair, her clothes hunched around her. The chair was too low and increasing age made her body difficult to manage.

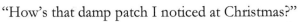

"How's that damp patch I noticed at Christmas?"

Kate was in the kitchen so Lydia needed to raise her voice to be heard above the chugging of the kettle. She was concerned about Kate and her family and tried not to let it show for fear of being accused of interfering.

"In the bathroom?" Kate called. Now Lydia was concerned that there were other problems with other ceilings. "Don't know. Haven't checked. Too much else to worry about."

"What do you mean? Has something happened?"

"Dan's been made redundant."

Lydia drew in her breath. "Did you say 'redundant'?"

Kate elbowed her way into the room, carrying a loaded tray which she placed on a side table. She straightened, rubbing her lower back. Kate, with curly dark hair, took after her father. It was Ellie, tall, fair, who favoured Lydia, once, herself, fair but now common-or-garden grey.

"Last week," she said. "Just like that. The whole firm. Not just his branch. A phone call. That's all, a phone call, after the years he's been there. That's what it's like, now, Dan says. The paperwork follows. There is no demand for traditional furniture stores any more, what with the internet and out-of-town shopping centres."

"Kate, I'm so sorry. What a shock. What a worry. Does he get redundancy money?"

"Not been there long enough. You know what he's like, doesn't stay anywhere very long. Always changing jobs."

"Is there anything I can do? Why didn't you tell me?"

"It's all right." Kate recoiled visibly at the sympathy.

"He's got another job. It doesn't pay as well, though. He's in the big supermarket."

"Doing what?"

"A bit of everything. He's sold the car. No need to worry. But I'm afraid there won't be a lift home tonight. He'll be much later, too."

"That's a minor detail. I can get the bus. Or walk. All the same, I wish…" Kate would know what Lydia wished and would refuse it so fiercely. Lydia watched her. She looked older than forty-four. Her body conveyed weariness, her hair was straggly, her face pale. Lydia knew the situation. It had not begun last week with Dan's redundancy. They had always had money problems. The once pretty child was now an over-burdened housewife and mother. A wave of sorrow swept over Lydia. She must accept that she had been unable to prevent this happening to her eldest daughter. How could she have done anything?

"I don't know how you cope with this modern world, you youngsters," Lydia said.

"Youngster? Me? Thanks, Mum. I was sure my emotional maturity was the only compensation for being forty-four."

A key grated and rattled in the front door lock. Their faces expectant, mother and daughter heard the door being shut with care, a rustling of clothes followed by faint thumps as shoes were trodden off feet and tossed aside. Polly, in socks, appeared in the doorway of the sitting room.

"Hi, Mum. Hello, Gran. I didn't expect to see you here."

Polly, nearly sixteen, a young version of Kate, had brought a frisson of energy, a lightness, into the room.

Lydia held out her arms to her. "Hello, dear. How are you?"

"I'm great, Gran. You?"

"I'm great, too, dear."

"Have you got homework?" Kate said. She didn't wait for an answer. "You should do it now rather than put it off until you want to watch telly. You know what happens. You put it off and put it off..."

Lydia expected, even hoped, Polly would resist this, but she smiled at Lydia and obediently left the room.

"She's clever," Kate said. "I don't want her slacking." Kate was driven and she drove, too.

Lydia gave attention to the scarf arranged around her neck, hanging to conceal her lumpy figure. Poor Polly, pushed into doing what she didn't want to do. The room was gloomier without her presence.

"She's a good girl," Kate said, as if trying to convince Lydia of something.

"I can see." Not a bit like her mother was at that age. Polly was in danger of having the light squashed out of her if Kate did not relax. "Not a typical adolescent, clearly."

"There's time." Kate was so glum, as if adolescence was an illness, or an infection, not a necessary stage of growing up. Lydia gazed around as Kate poured tea. Once fashionable and furnished with pride, the sitting room was looking uncared for and worn. Cushions were shapeless, curtains pulled back rashly, the carpet threadbare in places. There were stains from spilled tea and coffee on the upholstery. The windows needed cleaning. A layer of dust could be seen even in the dim light of a dull January afternoon.

"How's school?" Lydia asked.

"Hectic. I wish I'd become a teacher. I'm as good as

7

most of them with the kids. Instead, I'm a mere teaching assistant."

"I don't know why…"

"Because you wouldn't let me," Kate flared, sitting forward and speaking loudly. "That's why."

"That's not how I remember it."

"Of course not. You were too wrapped up in that hideous Peter Grover. How you stayed married to him all those years, I don't know." Kate was always touchy about Peter. Even now, she held the torch for her father, Mike.

Lydia refrained from her usual response to this old accusation. It was true that she had been in love with Peter Grover, had stayed with him for that reason. His death had caused her terrible grief for which neither of her daughters had offered comfort. She drew the conversation to Ellie, her other daughter.

"Have you seen Ellie recently?"

Kate seemed to relax and sat back in her chair. "No, I haven't. Have you?"

"Not since Christmas."

"She's busy."

"I haven't seen much of her at all in recent months," Lydia said, unable to hide a wistfulness in her voice.

"She has a right to her own life."

Lydia sighed. Kate wanted an argument. "Of course she has. But, you know, Ellie, she's a disappointment to me, that's all." Lydia was hoping that Kate would understand that *she* was not a disappointment to her.

Kate took a long sip from her mug of tea. "Mum, has it occurred to you that you are a disappointment to Ellie?"

"You mean because I'm not happy about the endless

stream of men she's had in her life?" Or was it because of one man in her own life that she might be a disappointment, still, to Ellie?

Kate was annoyed. Her face drooped and she frowned. "You are a prude, Mum."

Lydia wriggled in her uncomfortable chair. Rising from it would be difficult. Ageing was bringing loss of dignity, slowly but surely. And this visit was not going well.

The door was pushed open to reveal Polly, bringing light and life back into the room.

"Have you done that beastly homework?" Lydia asked smiling.

"You haven't done your homework already?" Kate said. "You haven't had time."

Polly ignored her mother's question, having given a nod in Lydia's direction. "Can I have some tea? Nick's got a girlfriend."

Kate looked up at her. Lydia watched. At nearly sixteen, Polly was still a child. She had none of the attributes of the teenage grandchildren of other people. Polly was unsophisticated, not concerned with fashion, not involved with new technology. She dreamed ballet, cats and read historical novels.

"About time," Kate said and Lydia wondered what the hurry was.

"Is she nice?" Lydia asked.

"Dunno."

"Then why mention it?" Kate said.

Polly shrugged, said, "Dunno," again and began to chatter about her new maths teacher. "He's lovely," she said. "So kind and he doesn't shout and that stops the boys shouting. I've moved my seat to the front to be nearer him. Where I sat before, Jane kept talking to me so I couldn't concentrate. It's better away from her, at the front." The maths teacher was 'out of this world', not for his teaching skills, not for his mathematical knowledge, but for his looks.

Kate did not respond to Polly's eulogy. She seemed to be preoccupied. They must have serious money problems, Kate and Dan, Lydia decided, recalling the damp patch on the bathroom ceiling and noting that the house was not warm enough for January. Even if they hadn't had money problems before, they surely would after Dan being made redundant. Lydia could have helped them, to a small extent, but previous offers of help had been rejected, and rejected angrily.

"Come up to my bedroom, Gran," Polly said when Lydia had almost finished her mug of tea.

"Gran's seen your room," Kate said, "at Christmas."

"You can see it again, can't you, Gran?"

"Of course." Lydia heaved herself out of the chair, glad to leave Kate and her negativity.

"That chair's too low, isn't it?" Polly said, impatiently shifting from one foot to the other. She led the way upstairs, pausing a few times to look back to check that Lydia followed, then, once in the bedroom, kicked off her slippers and threw herself onto her bed.

"That's a lovely bedspread," Lydia said, sinking into the only chair.

"I know. I'm not supposed to sit on it. Royal blue. My slippers are royal blue, too. I'm not supposed to do this, either." She pointed to her toes, wriggling them to draw attention to the red varnished nails.

Lydia smiled. She glanced round the room, wondering what she had been brought up to see.

10

"Gran, if I ask you something, will you promise to tell me the truth?"

So there was a reason, but not a visible one. "Yes, of course. What is it you want to ask?" Was it a personal question, or a question about her mother? Perhaps a question about the past, Mum as a girl, or did you have a Gran and was it a long time ago? Questions the grandchildren never asked but which Lydia would have loved to answer.

"Gran, am I fat?"

Lydia gazed at her, first in disappointment, then in puzzlement. "Why, no, dear, not at all. Why do you ask? Has someone said you are?"

Polly nodded, eyelids lowered. "You know I said about Jane? She's with Cordelia's crowd now. She said I'm fat with small—b'zooms. And she's getting Cordelia and her friends to say it."

"B'zooms?"

"We say b'zooms in my class, the girls. 'Tits' is what the boys say. Now Dad's been made redundant, I'll never be able to afford breast implants, or even chicken fillets."

"Chicken fillets?"

"You tuck them in your bra, to make you look bigger. They're plastic, or something."

"Your thinking is all wrong, Polly. There's nothing wrong with you. I'd say there's something wrong with the other girls." Lydia had wanted to smile but this was not a smiling matter. Tears hovered on the brims of Polly's innocent, hazel eyes. The matter was more serious even than Lydia had understood.

"Of course you're not fat. Your b'zooms will grow bigger. Honestly. Like your Mum's did. Have you spoken to Mum about your worry?"

"Yes, she just said I was not to be silly. But I think I am fat. I feel fat."

"Kate was about your size at your age. And very flat-chested."

"Mum was?"

"Yes. Really."

"I don't like Cordelia."

That sounded more like the real problem. "There must be some good news in your life, Polly. When you came in after school, it was as though the place lit up."

"Mr Hornby is the good news. That's why I moved my seat, you know. I mean, maths is maths, but Mr Hornby is something else. Where I sit now, I can smell him, his shower gel, his aftershave, whatever." She threw herself back on her pillows and gazed into a distance filled by Mr Hornby, a smile on her face. "He looks good, he sounds good, he smells good, and by God, he does me good."

Downstairs, the front door slammed. Nick knew no other way of dealing with doors. Lydia, having had two daughters, did not understand sons, or grandsons.

"I'm home!" Nick bellowed his arrival.

"I think your brother's home," Lydia said. "We should go down."

"Don't say a word to Mum, will, you about - about fat?"

"Of course not."

They went downstairs, Polly first. Kate was in the hall. She tilted her face towards Nick for a kiss. Nick obliged, greeted Lydia before he ambled into the kitchen, a pair of football boots dangling by their laces from his fastidious fingers. He was oblivious of the lumps of mud falling off them. Lydia and Polly followed at Kate's invitation. The kitchen was the warmest room in the house.

"I might give it up," he said as he stuffed the football kit into the washing machine.

"What, washing your kit?" Kate said.

"Yeah. And football. It's cold this time of year." He was turning knobs with confidence. The machine grumbled to a start.

"It was cold this time of year last year," Kate said.

"It's just not my religion," he said. He paused by the conservatory door, about to put his football boots out there to dry. "Ugh! Not shepherd's pie again? Are we hard up again?"

"There's no 'again'. We're always hard up." But Nick was not interested in why they were always hard up. He left the kitchen to stomp his way upstairs.

"Nick's got a girl friend," Polly said quietly when he'd gone.

Kate paused, hovering over the dishwasher. "Has he really?"

"He's old enough." Polly waited for a reaction and cast a sideways look at Lydia.

"Old enough?" Kate straightened. "For what?"

"Aw, Mum. Don't be so old-fashioned. Honestly! Get a life!"

"Do you know this girl?"

"I don't have anything to do with sixth-formers. Don't tell him I told you."

"Dan doesn't come in till much later now, Mum," Kate said. "We don't wait for him. Polly and Nick have to do their homework. Is it all right for you to eat this early?"

Get a life, Lydia thought. What an apt expression.

That was what she must do. She must get a life, or at least, get her life back. Now. Before it was too late. But how?

* * *

"I must be going," Lydia said, after the meal. She was restless. She needed to be on her own, to think. There was nothing else to talk about here. Kate was increasingly tense. These visits to her were always a let-down. Her daughters were her reason for living. What else was there? The grandchildren, Nick and Polly, were growing up and away fast. She must cease seeing her family as a way of negotiating the outside world, which she had never faced alone. Always there had been someone, her mother, then the girls' father, Mike, then Peter. Now the only ones left were Kate, who was grumpy and Ellie, who was busy.

"It's dark and it's raining," Lydia added to explain her earlier than usual departure.

"Aw, Gran, get a life," Polly said again.

Get a life, indeed, Lydia thought. About time, after five years.

"Don't be cheeky," Kate said.

Polly's grin vanished. "I'll come with you. To the bus stop, I mean."

"Oh, I thought you meant you'd come with me to get a life," Lydia said with a laugh and Polly's grin returned.

"We both will," Kate said. "I don't like to think of you standing there in the dark and the wet, all alone…"

Lydia smiled at that, but she could have cried at Kate's words. Kindness from her was so rare.

As the three of them left the house, Kate pulled the door closed behind them. It gave a faint click, a final sound. That was it, the visit. The night was wet and raw. They scurried along the pavement. A bus was approaching before they reached the stop. Kate hailed it.

"By the way, the snowdrops are out again," Lydia said as she hauled herself up onto the bus. She waved her bus pass at the driver, the same young black woman on whose bus she had arrived.

"Good visit?" she asked with an infectious smile to which Lydia responded.

"Medium," Lydia said. "I think I expect too much."

"Either that, or not enough. Same dilemma as me."

"Difficult, isn't it, to know which."

"They never even drop a hint!"

The bus hummed along, swishing through the wet night. Lydia pondered the conundrum of her daughters, Ellie, so happy but breaking all the rules, Kate, keeping the rules but having the appearance of being depressed.

The traffic paused outside Tarascon Court, flats for the over-sixties. Through the misty windows of the bus, the glowing panes of the five storey block gave an impression of being a harbour of warmth and safety. Veronica, an acquaintance, lived there. As the bus moved off again, Lydia's thoughts took a different direction. She could see a 'for sale' board in the garden, tantalising, challenging in its absurd synchronicity.

Reaching her stop, she said 'goodnight' to the driver who bade her to 'take care, now'. Head bowed, she almost ran, as much as running was possible for her, along the pavement and round the corner to her house. Banal as she thought such a sentiment was, to her, one of the worst aspects of ageing was her inability to run.

Her body would only respond with sluggishness to the commands she gave it.

The house loomed, a large detached house, modern with four bedrooms, three of which were rarely used in the five years since Peter died. Tonight, as she trod the paved drive, she was admitting that the house was more than she could manage, more than she needed. Sentimentality had caused her to resist any notion of selling but now common sense was urging her to consider it. She unlocked the front door. Not for the first time the silence, the darkness, as she stepped inside, threatened her peace of mind. Her true perceptions were beginning to surface. No longer was she feeling the need to cling so fiercely to her past. It would be almost impossible to let go completely. How did other people of her age manage such a drastic change? She might phone Veronica.

Once a thought had occurred, it could not be unthought. The idea of selling the house kept returning to her, as did the memories of happy times there. She was having a tug of war with herself, and war was the significant word.

She glanced at the calorie content of the meal heating up in the microwave, and wished she hadn't. No wonder she was putting on weight. Loneliness and boredom were relieved by food. Again, her mind returned to the possibility of selling the house, this lovely house, with its garden. The thought made her feel queasy. Tonight was choir practice night. This was her only outside activity. The wind howled round the house, there was a storm brewing. The worry lingered, as always, that there might be damage to the property if the wind increased and the rain continued. She was reminded of Kate and the problem with the roof over her bathroom. Poor Kate. Lydia was really sorry for her. What trouble she and Dan were in.

She was so absorbed in her thoughts that the ready-meal passed her lips without her taste buds recognition. She made a decision, one that did not involve any commitment, but would enable her to gather more information. Choir practice could be given a miss tonight. She located her phone to tap out the number of Veronica, who lived at Tarascon Court.

"Come round on Friday," Veronica said. "Ten-thirty."

* * *

Veronica 's flat was number nineteen Tarascon Court. She was hardly a friend, more properly she was a mere acquaintance. They had met in the doctor's waiting room, just a few years ago and subsequently encountered each other while shopping. A habit had grown of having coffee together.

Lydia now pressed the digits on the entry-phone and a refined voice responded to tell her to take the lift to the fourth floor.

When she stepped out of the lift Veronica was waiting at her front doorway. In contrast to Lydia's height, simplicity and her preference for black, Veronica was a slight figure, dressed in pastel greens and blues, her dyed blonde hair piled high and rigid. She sported much sparking jewellery, earrings, rings, a bracelet. Her make-up was a work of art. Her demeanour expressed delicacy. She was not Lydia's type, but ageing restricted choice. Friends diminished when you were older, they died, became ill or frail, or moved away. Lydia had made very few new ones.

She was served coffee and almond biscuits in an over-furnished flat, brimming with memorabilia and with a stunning view across the town from a big picture window.

"This is lovely," Lydia said, going over to the window. "It gives you a great feeling of freedom."

"And it's quiet," Veronica said. "No children. Warm in winter. I love it here. Come and look round."

The flat was more spacious than Lydia had anticipated, consisting of the living room, a kitchen, a main bedroom, a second bedroom, which was much smaller, and a bathroom that was fitted with a shower and grab rails and a high toilet seat. The rooms, each with emergency cords to summon help in case of accident or illness, were arranged around a small hall with storage spaces.

"When you leave a bigger place," Veronica explained, "you bring a lot with you. You need somewhere to store life's accumulation."

"I suppose so." Lydia observed that much of Veronica's accumulation was displayed on her walls, every flat surface being crammed with ornaments, lamps, bric-a-brac. Her chairs were recliners.

"Sue, the manager here, is lovely," said Veronica. "I don't mix with the neighbours very much. Most of them are not my sort, you understand. They're pleasant enough, though."

Lydia avoided an exchange about the neighbours. "Did you have doubts about coming here?"

"Oh, no," Veronica said.

Lydia gazed at her in disbelief. Was it possible not to have regrets, leaving a home of years, succumbing to ageing?

"I was relieved, really, from all the worry of my bungalow. But that was before I had a retirement flat in London. I kept having to call on my son to do repairs and things. I've only got the one son, you see, to help me. You're lucky. You have two daughters."

Where luck came into the equation, Lydia could not see. Her daughters were living their own lives, they had their own concerns. Depending on them for practical help and emotional support was not an option, especially not Kate, who had her two children and a host of problems.

"Why did you move down here?"

"My son suggested it. He had already moved here and he wanted me to be near him."

"Where is the empty flat, Veronica, do you know?"

"On the top floor. It has views across the other side of the town." Veronica paused. "Do you think you might like to move in?"

"I really don't know. It needs some consideration."

"You should discuss it with your daughters. I discussed it with my son."

There were several reasons for perceiving that as a bad idea. She might, however, in one way or another, involve Polly. After more almond biscuits than were good for her, Lydia rose to leave.

As she stepped out of the lift to leave the building, a voice called her name.

"Lydia? Yes, it is you. Lydia!"

She turned. Coming towards her from the main door was Clive Morris, a tenor in the choir. He was a quiet, balding man with a neat moustache. He always wore a blazer.

"Hello, Clive. Do you live here?"

19

"I do, indeed. How nice to see you. What are you doing here?"

"I've been to see a friend, Veronica Hornby. Do you know her?"

"Veronica? Yes. I know her. I think she's in the flat below me. You're not by any chance, thinking of moving in here, are you?"

"Well," Lydia hesitated, "I don't know. Not yet."

"There's a vacant flat on the top floor, on the same corridor as mine."

"You're on the top floor?"

"Number twenty-five."

Lydia took two steps towards Clive. "How long have you lived here?"

"Oh, must be nearly two years now."

"Did you have doubts before you made the decision?" She noticed that the badge on the breast pocket of his blazer was that of the local bowls club.

"Good grief, no. It was what I needed. Haven't looked back since." He paused, with a smile. "It would be nice if you were to move in."

Being wanted was always flattering. She smiled. "I don't know, Clive. I really don't. I wonder if I would be better off in a small bungalow."

He looked disappointed. "You didn't go to choir practice Wednesday night, did you?"

"The weather was terrible."

"The church and the church hall are just round the corner from here. Easy to slip out, whatever the weather." With a laugh and a wave of the hand he strode towards the lift. "See you at choir next week," he called as the doors closed.

After she left Tarascon Court, Lydia aimed, on foot,

for the town where she had a light lunch at her favourite cafe, Claire's Tea Rooms. Her appetite was diminished, for what she was about to do she had hitherto refused to consider. She planned to visit an estate agent with a view to obtaining a valuation on, and possibly selling, her house. The estate agency was the one selling the top floor flat at Tarascon Court and it was the local branch of the chain her late husband, Peter Grover, had owned.

The young man in the estate agency, Ryan, was helpful. He would visit the property on Monday morning, he said.

"Would I have difficulty selling?" she asked him, "at this time of the year?" Some years had passed since she had been employed in the estate agency and a lot had happened since then with regard to the buying and selling on the property market.

"Gracehill? No trouble at all," he replied. "In fact, there was a couple in only last week asking if we had anything in that area. I had to disappoint them. I can get in touch with them again, of course. Would you like me to come and give a valuation on Monday?"

Lydia then asked for particulars of the flat at Tarascon Court. She studied the printed details he gave her. An appointment was made to view it on Tuesday afternoon.

"If I sold my house easily," she said, "how long would the conveyancing take?"

"It depends. But if you are in a hurry and have a co-operative solicitor, no complications, it could be done in six weeks, even less."

"Six weeks." She stood gazing into space. The quicker the better. Prolonging the agony would allow doubts to creep in. "If I'm going to do it, it's got to be quick or I'll lose my nerve."

"I understand," he said. "It can be daunting, moving to a retirement scheme. But Tarascon Court does seem a contented place."

"My solicitor would certainly be co-operative. He was my late husband's friend."

The omens were auspicious.

* * *

She left the estate agents' office feeling weak. How had she done this! She took her walk home slowly, deep in thought most of the time. As she reached the gateway of the house, she paused to try to see the place in the eyes of a prospective purchaser. In the winter's afternoon sunshine it looked snug and almost smiling, with its horizontal lines, soft curves and round bays.

She let herself in and made a cup of tea. Cup and saucer in hand, she wandered round the house. The sun was beginning to dip low, casting a glow in the lounge that gave its pale decor some colour. She and Peter had decorated and furnished this room with love and care. Nothing had been altered in the time since he had died. The softness about the room, nothing really to do with its upholstery, reflected the man. He had been a gentle and caring person. Her girls had despised him for what they saw as a lack of manliness. But whatever his qualities, he would have been criticised as the man who was taking their father's place in their mother's life. Kate and Ellie had been unmerciful in their treatment of him. He had borne it stoically, patiently. Even after their father Mike had died, they did not relent.

Still seeing her home from the point of view of a purchaser, she roamed from room to room. The dining room, never used now, was simple in its elegance. The breakfast room, next to the kitchen, was the room she lived in, her snug, with its comfortable furnishings, television and out-of-date music centre.

Returning to the kitchen, she left her cup and saucer on the draining board, turned to survey this part of the house. Old-fashioned maybe, it had been the vogue twenty-five years ago. The Aga would appeal. She opened cupboard doors. One cupboard was stacked with china, untouched since before Peter died. She should let Kate and Ellie have that.

Her survey took her upstairs. There were four bedrooms here, all lovingly furnished and decorated, three of them hardly ever occupied except for the odd occasion when Polly came to stay the night. The single bed that Polly used on these occasions could come with her to Tarascon Court, for the small bedroom.

With reluctance, she ventured into the master bedroom. Since she had been alone she hadn't slept in here. Peter's framed photograph stood on the bedside table on her side of the bed. On Peter's side was a photograph taken on their wedding day, she in pale blue, he looking spruced and smiling. Hunched together on one side were Kate and Ellie, their faces blank. Little did they, even now, realise the pain they had caused. She knew of their pain about the slow and considered leaving of their father and the family home, for she recalled the time her own mother had done something similar.

She sat down on the bed and picked up the photograph of Peter, tracing the smiling eyes with her forefinger. Sorrow washed over her, consumed her, as though all the deeper grief of the last years, often resisted, had been unleashed and gathered at this one point in time. She fell onto the bed and wept, her tears staining the silk duvet cover, until she slept, exhausted.

Much later the persistent ringing of the doorbell roused her. It was dark now. She raised her head in alarm, confused as to where she was. Remembering, she sat bolt upright. Her awareness of her vulnerable position as an older woman, alone in the big house, in darkness, caused her heart to pound. Who could be at the door at this hour?

She hurried down the staircase. Someone was peering through the letterbox.

"Mum! It's me, Kate."

Kate was cold when she came in. Lydia, still confused, took time to try to understand the purpose of this visit, especially as she had seen her daughter as recently as last Tuesday.

"Is there something wrong, Kate?" she asked.

"No-o." The upturned end of the short word conveyed defiance. So something was wrong. "I'm fine. Why are you sleeping at this time? It's not long after half-past seven. You don't look well."

"I'm fine," Lydia said. Part of her wished she could confide in her daughter, but she didn't trust her in her present mood. There was hostility in her tone and manner which could create a barrier between them.

"I've come to invite you to a family lunch party, on Sunday week. At our place. Everyone, including Ellie." She went into details about the time, the place and who would be there. "You, me, Ellie, Dan, and Nick and Polly. It'll be like Christmas again, without all the glitter and expense."

Why now, so soon after Christmas? Lydia wondered.

Her phone left on the table, rang. It was Dan, demanding to know if Kate was there.

"Yes, she is, Dan. Do you want to speak to her?"

"No, I'll speak to her when she comes home. I'll have a lot to say. She's switched off her phone. I didn't know where she was. There was no need for her to run off like that. I don't know what's the matter with her, moody cow. Tell her to get back here asap or she'll find the door locked."

"How did you know she was here?"

"I tried Ellie. She's not at home, though. After that, there was only you. Tell her to get back here." The phone went dead.

"That was Dan, wasn't it? What did he say?"

Lydia quoted verbatim what Dan had said.

Kate avoided looking at her. "I guess I'd better go, then."

Kate had stayed less than half an hour. She looked thoroughly wretched. The family meal would take place on Sunday week, at two o'clock, to fit in with Dan's shift work. Kate, or Ellie, could have phoned with the invitation. There was no need to walk all the way to Lydia's house. Not much detective work was required to deduce that Kate and Dan had had a row. Lydia had a strong intuition, too, that this might be an occasion for Ellie to announce yet again that she had found 'Mr Right'.

Lydia might have her own news to impart.

* * *

Ryan, the estate agent, visited on Monday afternoon. His valuation of the house astonished Lydia.

"That much?" she said. "I *am* out of touch. There's

room to play with, isn't there? I mean, if I'm willing to drop the price a bit for a speedy transaction –".

He smiled. "There'll be no need for that, I'm pretty sure."

They sat in the lounge after the tour of the house. He paused before continuing. "The couple I mentioned to you, on Friday, they are very keen to view."

Lydia gazed at him. She had contemplated these plans all week-end, preparing herself for a glitch. But everything was running smoothly, as if it was meant. She smiled to herself, fantasising that Peter might be influencing events from another realm. Believing that would help her to feel easier about the decision.

"I'll make up my mind finally when I've had a look at the flat tomorrow afternoon," she said. "Of course, I could leave much of the furniture if they wished. All I'll need is my bed, a table. Everything else I could buy at a leisurely pace afterwards."

"Charity shops are pretty keen to have quality furniture," he said.

Oh, dear, destruction of the happy home. A note of discord had been struck. It could cause her to lose her nerve.

She saw the flat at two o'clock the next afternoon. A floor higher than Veronica's, and like Veronica's, two-bedroomed but empty of furnishings, she was able to appreciate the opportunity before her.

"Yes, I want this," she said, her voice, her manner, calm, in contrast to what was going on inside her, a churning of her thoughts, of her stomach. Yet, despite all that, there was a near certainty that this really must be right. For how long, she wondered, would she, could she, be certain that it was right?

She walked back to her home. As she entered the porch and was about to unlock the front door ,when a movement beside her caused her to call out. Someone was curled up in the corner of the porch. That someone was revealed to be Polly.

"My dear child," gasped Lydia, "what are you doing there? Why are you not at school?"

Polly, as she scrambled to her feet, burst into tears.

"You'd better come indoors," Lydia said. "Look at your school clothes, all covered in dirt." She wanted to mother the girl, make her feel cared for. She led her to the kitchen where she was dusted down, seated at the table and presented with tea and biscuits.

"Tell me," Lydia said, sitting opposite her, "what's happened?"

"I haven't been to school today." Polly sniffed. "I didn't want to see Mrs Hawkins." She raised tragic eyes to Lydia's. "I'm innocent."

"Of what?"

"Of punching Cordelia on the nose and making it bleed. Mrs Hawkins thinks I did. I was supposed to see her this morning. But I didn't go. I didn't do it, you see."

"Then how did this Cordelia get a bloody nose?"

"She and the others were trying to give me a tattoo. With a needle and some coloured stuff, ink, I think. In the girls' toilets. They grabbed me. I yelled and flayed my arms around, trying to stop them. They held me here." She indicated her upper arms. She glanced up at Lydia. "Cordelia, she's the one who calls me fat."

Poor Polly. Lydia heard this in alarm, wanting to protect her from these loutish girls.

"And you haven't told Kate about this? The tattooing and calling you fat?"

"No. And I couldn't go home because Dad's there till two. He does a different shift this week. Then I tried Ellie's. She had someone there, talking wedding dresses. That was after the library. I went there first, but they got suspicious of me so I came out. Then, in the end, I came here. But you were out."

"Have you had any lunch?"

"No. But I'm okay."

"Well, I don't think so. Have a sandwich."

"In a minute."

"Why haven't you told your Mum about this bullying?"

"Because she's got problems. They had a row on Friday, she and Dad did, and they haven't forgiven each other yet. It's horrible at home. Dad did the shopping on Friday because he's at the Supermarket and he said it would save time for Mum. He gets a discount, too. But he spent more than he should have done. Mum was cross because he'd got ready-meals."

"I expect he was trying to save Mum a bit of time."

"Well, they won't because she threw a packet of chicken Jalfrezi at him. It missed, but the Tandoori chicken didn't. Then he told her he'd got it all on the credit card and that's no good, she said, because they'd agreed not to use it for food."

Lydia hurriedly prepared a cheese sandwich for her.

"There's going to be a bit of news on Sunday," Polly said, watching the sandwich preparation. "I don't know what it is but they were talking, Mum and Ellie on the phone."

"Really? That's interesting because I might have some news, too."

"What?"

28

"You'll see. I want you to tell your Mum about the bullying."

"No way." Polly shook her head and passed her hand before her, palm faced out.

"If you don't, I'll have to."

"You wouldn't dare. You wouldn't betray me. I'll never share a secret with you again, if you do."

Lydia had to take the risk. Kate would be furious at even the suggestion that she was keeping Polly's serious problems from her. "Wouldn't dare, wouldn't I?"

Polly slumped back in her chair.

Lydia rose to come round the table, intending to embrace her. She caught hold of her by the arm, to persuade her to sit up and take the whole matter seriously. Polly yelped.

"What's the matter?"

"That's my bad arm."

"Bad arm? What happened to it?"

"The girls. I told you."

"Let me see."

Polly removed her sweater and the left sleeve of her blouse. Lydia gasped in shock. "Those are very nasty bruises, Polly. I can see the marks of fingers there. You must tell Mum. It's a pity you didn't see that teacher and show her these."

Polly twisted her head to see the back of her upper arm. "I didn't know they were that bad." She looked up at Lydia. "Why would I want to show them to Mrs Hawkins?"

"She'd believe you if you did. She wouldn't be so quick to believe your friend."

"Cordelia? She's no friend." Polly adjusted her clothes. "Perhaps I should go home and wait for Mum and then tell her. Can I take my sarnie with me?"

"I think that's an excellent idea, going home to tell your Mum. Yes, take your sarnie."

Polly gathered together her school bag and coat and appeared to be gathering her thoughts. She became quiet, without looking at Lydia.

"I'll go now," she said. "I'll be there when Mum comes in. Thanks, Gran."

She said goodbye, aiming for the front door. Lydia hurried after her.

"I might be able to take you out for lunch on Saturday," she said.

"Cool," Polly said raising a briefly smiling face. "I'd like that."

Lydia watched from the open front door as Polly hastened towards the gate, and with a wave, turned left in the direction of her home.

* * *

The couple mentioned by Ryan, came to view the house on Wednesday afternoon. They traipsed through the rooms, giving nothing away, their faces impassive, their lips sealed. They asked few questions, but lingered in every room. They spent a long time in the garden. Lydia was tempted to mention the snowdrops. She would want them preserved, respected even. They would not be able to go with her, if she moved. Always, every thought was qualified by that little word 'if'. The couple left, thanking her for her time and the inconvenience. There was no hint that, later that afternoon, Ryan would telephone to say they had made an offer, just below the asking price. Lydia decided to play it cool and refrained from making a response. Doubts were setting in, not about the wisdom of the plan, but due to the sentimental pull of the home that had been hers and Peter's. It was the snowdrops.

All evening she fought memories of her twenty years in the house with Peter and the five years since he died. She could not settle. Immersing herself in a television programme failed. The possibility of a quick visit to Kate or Ellie might have settled her qualms but the prospect of Sunday's lunch party and anticipating telling and receiving news inhibited her. She went to bed early and spent a night wakeful and tense. Would she know who she was without the status of the house in the best part of town? How would she cope with being like 'everyone else', those mythical creatures who, in her youth, and even later, she had determined to emulate. Her marriage to Mike, her first husband and the girls' father, had been a result of that. Such a mistake, wrong motive, wrong man.

Polly's lunch with her was arranged, by phone, for Saturday at Claire's Tea Rooms in the smartest end of town. When Polly arrived, Lydia had a surprise. The girl's appearance had altered. She was unrecognisable. Her hair was piled in a fetching topknot on her head. Irritating thin locks of hair hung at the side of her face. She wore make up and long earrings that sparkled in the winter sun.

She sat down with a grin. "What?" she said, her challenging tone a response to her grandmother's raised eyebrows and broad smile.

"You look really lovely, Polly," Lydia said.

"Thanks, Gran. Mum was cross. She said I was tarted up. I said, 'for God's sake, I'm sixteen in the summer. Don't you think I should look it?' She just grunted."

Today, Polly did look as though she would be sixteen in the summer and she behaved that way too. Until today she had appeared much younger than her age with her gaucheness, her enthusiasms and her casual clothes.

"You were right about telling Mum about the bruises," she said.

"Of course I was."

"Mrs Hawkins, the teacher, spoke to me. Actually, I went back to school when I left you. I wouldn't have slept if I'd had it hanging over me all night. Mrs Hawkins spoke to Cordelia and the other girls. And she sent a letter home to Mum."

"What did Mum say?"

"She was cross. With me."

"For not telling her that?"

"No, for being in trouble. But I wasn't, not really."

"I think your Mum's got a lot of worry lately. Try to understand."

"Yeah. But when's she going to understand me?" She took out her smart phone.

"What are you doing?" Lydia asked as Polly began to fiddle with it.

"It's my phone. Jez showed me things on it I didn't know."

"Who's Jez?"

"A boy in my class." Polly grinned. "He said he could give me some good PR."

"What's that?"

"That's what I said. Public relations. In class, he said. Cordelia's putting it about that I'm violent. He said he doesn't believe her. I'm too quiet, he said."

"I see. Put the phone away now. Eat your lunch," Lydia said, "After this I want to take you somewhere that will surprise you. But I would like you to keep quiet about it all until the lunch party tomorrow. Is that agreeable?"

"I only wanted to show you my bullying diary. That was Jez's idea. To write things down, record what they do to me, those girls. The thing is they leave me alone now. So I just do a diary. Tell me about the secret." She tucked her phone in her pocket and clasped her hands together, her enthusiasm showing through the new image. "Yes, I'll keep mum. I won't say a word. What is it?"

"You'll see."

* * *

Ryan was waiting in the hallway at Tarascon Court.

"This is my grand-daughter, she's come to advise me," Lydia said.

"Lydia!" Clive Morris was hurrying from the lift. "Have you decided?"

"I'm not sure, Clive. You know, the marital home…"

Clive nodded. "I consider I did the right thing. I look forward to seeing you here. And seeing you this Wednesday, at the choir."

Ryan was waiting. Eyebrows raised in query, Polly stepped into the lift. Her eyes were dancing with pleasure at the prospect of being let in on a secret. Lydia smiled her own delight.

"Who was that?" Polly whispered.

"Clive? He's in the choir. A tenor." They followed Ryan along the corridor on the top floor.

"Who's he?" Polly whispered again, gazing at Ryan this time.

"He's an estate agent. From Peter's estate agency."

Polly's eyebrows shot higher.

Ryan unlocked the door of number twenty-nine and stood aside to allow them to enter. Lydia, watching Polly's face, stood back to let her in first. She hovered on the threshold.

"It's empty," she said stepping into the hall. She pushed open the living room door, her topknot wobbling in her excitement.

"Wow!" she said, though whether it was the size of the secret being shared with her, or the size of the flat compared with the house, Lydia was unsure. Polly gazed out of the living room window at the view of the town in the winter sunshine. She turned to Lydia.

"You're going to live here, aren't you?"

Lydia put her arm around her grand-daughter's shoulders. "Yes, dear, I think I might."

"Will you have enough space?"

"To do what?"

Polly shrugged. "Dunno. To sing?"

They both laughed.

"It's for older people, isn't it?"

"Why d'you say that?"

Polly pointed. "That red thing. You pull it if you die or something, don't you?" She giggled. "It's not a home, is it? You're not coming here because you are going ga-ga, are you?"

"It's a block of flats and it's managed by a manager who does the things the residents can't, because they are getting older, like organising lights in the corridor if they go out, and getting the lift repaired. Everyone is very independent, otherwise. A residential home is quite different," Lydia said.

"Oh. I was a bit worried." Polly investigated the kitchen, both bedrooms, the bathroom and the cupboards.

"What's the verdict?" Lydia said.

"I think it's lovely. I'd love flat like this. It's all you need, isn't it? And you'd be safe here. I'll worry now until you get here because I can see your house is big and lonely and if it was me, I'd be scared of burglars."

Lydia gave her another hug for saying the right thing. "We won't keep Ryan much longer. We'll go down to see my friend Veronica on the floor below."

"Will I be able to stay the night in that little bedroom?"

"Of course, if you want to."

"Oh, I'd love to."

Having thanked Ryan for his time, Lydia led Polly downstairs to number nineteen. She rang the doorbell. The door was opened briskly. By a man.

There was a gasp from Polly. Then she squealed, all her carefully constructed sophistication collapsed.

"Mr Hornby! It's Mr Hornby!" She clasped her hands under her chin, her face pink, eyes shining.

"Hello, Pauline."

Mr Hornby then addressed Lydia. "You must be Mum's friend…?"

"Lydia Grover," she finished for him, extending her hand. "This is my grand-daughter."

"I'm Ashton. Veronica's son." He held the door wide for them to enter.

"He's my teacher," Polly was saying, unable to address him directly. "My maths teacher."

Lydia exchanged amused glances with the handsome Mr Hornby. He was certainly a charmer. She had to admire Polly's taste.

35

Veronica appeared. "This is my son, Ashton. Ashie," said Veronica, "go and make some tea for us, will you? And what will you have, dear?" to Polly.

Ashie? As if the name Ashton was not already an embarrassment for the poor man. They were shown into Veronica's over-stuffed sitting room. Polly sat next to Lydia on a stool, perched upright. "I'll have tea, too, please." Her eyes followed Ashton Hornby as he went to the kitchen.

"He's my teacher," Polly claimed again, addressing Veronica.

Veronica smiled, and asked questions about Lydia's prospective sale and purchase. Polly sat gazing at the doorway waiting for Ashton Hornby to reappear. He brought in a tray of pretty china, cups and saucers, pale blue with pink roses. Lydia recounted the details of the property negotiations in the week and the likelihood of moving at the end of February.

"Oh," said Veronica, "half term's about then. Ashton will be around to help you if you need it."

Pert and prim on the edge of her seat, with her cup and saucer held carefully in her hands, Polly spoke for the first time since she had arrived, apart from saying 'he's my teacher.'

"I'll be able to help, too, Gran."

Lydia smiled indulgently. She must resist chaos at all costs.

Ashton appeared in the doorway. "I'll be going now, Mum," he said and stepped across the room to bestow a kiss on Veronica's delicate cheek, Polly's wide-eyed gaze still fixed on him. He left. Polly stared at the closed door after him. "He's my favourite teacher," she said with a sigh.

So Polly had discovered the opposite sex, this particular specimen safely out of reach, of course. Lydia approved of her choice.

"Gran," Polly said, as they were leaving Tarascon Court sometime later, "are you buying the flat?" She indicated the 'For Sale' board standing by the gateway.

Lydia agreed that she was.

"Are you selling your house?"

"I am, I think." Had a final, firm decision been made? There was still time to change her mind.

"Then do they cost the same? Because if it's so, it seems unbalanced, you know, small flat, big house. I don't know anything about buying houses."

Lydia stood still in the middle of the pavement. "Yes, there is a difference."

"Then what will you do with the difference?"

She drew a deep breath and prepared to tell a lie. Although she had no obvious reason to do so, some instinct prompted her. Money could complicate and confound relationships. She needed to be wanted for herself, not for her money. "You know what a mortgage is?"

"Borrowed money, isn't it?"

"I have a mortgage on the house. It has to be paid off."

"But there will be a little bit left over, won't there? I was thinking you'll need new curtains and things won't you?"

Lydia sighed in relief and gave a little laugh. Polly was a dear. She was pleased about the flat. Or was she pleased about Mr Hornby?

* * *

When she set out for Kate's house on Sunday, Lydia caught the bus. She was taking two bottles of wine with her. The young driver, who had previously been so friendly, was driving again.

"Are you in sole charge of this route?" Lydia asked as she tucked away her bus pass.

"I'm on it most week-ends. Where to this time?" she said.

"The same. Family. I've been invited to lunch, probably because I complained I don't see them enough."

"It paid off, then!"

"Actually, I don't think I had any influence at all. They tend to forget me. I'm too old to bother about."

"Aw! Don't say that. Maybe they're just immature."

"It's all relative, isn't it?"

"It's all relatives."

Lydia alighted and the driver called after her, "Bye. Have fun!"

"I intend to!" Lydia laughed. She was looking forward to surprising her daughters with her news. She hoped they would be as pleased for her as she was for herself. Never before had she done anything so daring, at least not since she had abandoned Mike, the girls' father, for Peter. Her heart did a flip as she recalled the way she had left him. This would not be as daring, as outrageous as that.

The meal was to begin at two o'clock to fit in with Dan's shifts at the supermarket. Ellie would be there. She had phoned Lydia briefly the evening before to confirm it.

Polly opened the door.

"Hi, Gran," she said, lifting her face to be kissed.

"You're wearing your posh fur coat. Can I try it on? Ellie's here."

Lydia slipped off her imitation fur coat for Polly to try on. "You haven't said anything, have you?"

"Not a whisper. Honestly. Don't tell about Jez, will you?"

"Who?"

"The boy in my class."

That was thoughtless, forgetting Polly's confidence. "Of course not. My lips are sealed."

Polly beamed. Kate emerged from the kitchen.

"Hello, dear," Lydia greeted her. "You're looking pink and flushed, can I do anything?" Her muffled voice came from the midst of hugs and kisses which always gave her the impression of being hurried. Kate was not comfortable with any hint of emotion.

"You're wearing that scent, aren't you, Mum?" she said, sniffing ostentatiously.

Lydia remembered. The scent was the one Peter used to buy for her. She had applied it out of habit. It went with the favourite outfit and the fur coat. Kate's comment, the tone of it, had all the feel of an accusation. Like the scent, the resentment of Peter had lingered.

"We're using the dining room today," Polly announced, standing in the doorway, swaddled in Lydia's coat. "We switched on the radiator," she lowered her voice, "'specially for you."

"You're looking glamorous," Lydia told her. She indicated Polly's long hair, brushed out and topped with the circle of small, pink, plastic rosebuds. She wore a long skirt.

"Borrowed from Mum," she said, holding it out to display its fullness.

39

Ellie was in the sitting room. Tall, slender, in a black sweater and trousers, she looked neat, her fair hair in a new short style and brushed off her face. She leapt to her feet as her mother came into the room. They hugged each other, Lydia wanting to hold onto her longer because she had seen so little of her recently.

"Are you okay, Mum?" Ellie said. She looked happy, radiant, even.

"I'm fine, dear. You?"

"Wonderful," Ellie said. She seemed to want to say more but changed her mind. "It's good to see you, Mum."

"I haven't seen you for ages, not since Christmas," Lydia said, unable to resist the observation as Ellie already began to move away from her. She tried to hang onto her, one hand slipping along Ellie's arm to her fingers as her daughter gently and gradually withdrew the grasp until only their fingers were loosely touching, then the connection was completely broken.

"I know. Busy enjoying life." Ellie said.

"Well, so am I, which would explain it, wouldn't it?" The up-beat comment disguised her disappointment.

"Listen, Mum, I have some news. I want to tell everyone when we're all together, sitting down for our meal."

"Good news, is it? You look as though it is. I have some news too." She was getting a life too, a new life, and it was difficult. She needed support in the decision she was making.

"Really? I can't wait for you to tell us."

Dismissed with the insincere words, Lydia had doubts that Ellie thought her mother's news was likely to be significant. Once past a certain age, you didn't really count, if being a mother ever counted, unless of course, you stopped behaving like the all-caring, all-suffering mother and wanted to 'get a life', as Polly had put it. When she had got a life, with Peter, the disapproval never waned.

Dan appeared, having changed into his old clothes now he had come home from work. Short and dark, he was never smart, even for visitors. He sloped about the house, hair dishevelled, slippers down at heel, as though he was in a dream. He greeted Lydia. She sat in one of the chairs that were low and uncomfortable. Her heart began to pound as tension built up in her. Doubts about her plans were magnifying. Was she doing this merely to be noticed by the family? This could be a new reason for abandoning the sale and purchase. She could summon a dozen other reasons. She must focus on the meal. Kate had gone to a lot of trouble. Herself and her agonising, she could analyse those later.

Redundancy or not, Kate and Dan had truly gone to town with this meal. Lydia hoped they had not got into debt in the process. Perhaps Ellie had helped out financially. She wished she had been asked to contribute. The meal was cassoulet. "Pork, duck and beans," Kate explained, "amongst other things."

"Beans make you…," Polly began.

"Polly!" Kate said.

Nick appeared, greeted Lydia with a kiss then everyone was asked to go to the dining room. Lydia found herself next Polly, much to the delight of both of them. She was anxious about telling her news and Polly would be an ally.

"This is lovely," Lydia said, regarding the meal before her.

"I'm not eating meat," Polly said.

"Why not?" Kate looked up.

"I'm vegetarian now."

"Get on with it," Kate told her.

When the meal was well underway, Ellie, across the table from Lydia, looked over to her.

"Mum has some news. Are you going tell us what it is, Mum? Are you ready, to tell?"

Placing her knife and fork on her plate, Lydia surveyed her audience. She took a deep breath. "I'm moving," she said.

They all gazed at her, as though they did not understand. Was it so unlikely?

"What, moving house?" Kate said.

"Where to?" Ellie said.

"I have a purchaser for the house and I'm moving to a flat."

"Flat?" Kate's face screwed up in disbelief. "A small one or a vast apartment?"

"A small one. Tarascon Court. Between here and the house."

"That's for old people," Kate said and the contempt in her voice was undisguised.

"It's a scheme of flats for retired people," Lydia said. "It's not a home. I'm nowhere near ready for that yet."

"Why?" Ellie said. "Why are you doing this?"

"The house is too big for me now. It's too lonely. I'm getting older. Perhaps you hadn't noticed."

"You're not old," Ellie protested, although as though the word was an insult or a failing.

Don't they see? Don't they see, the way she walked, the wrinkles, the slowness? Did they not consider each of her birthdays, for which they gave her elaborate cards, as a mark of time? Were they unable to compare every Christmas with the previous one?

"Have you had a good offer on the house?" Dan asked.

Under the table, on her lap, Lydia's hands began twisting round each other. This was what she feared. The arithmetic, especially Dan's arithmetic.. She must plan, make yet more decisions.

"Good enough," she said.

"Make sure you're not sold short," Dan went on. He liked money, was always full of good advice about it but never had any.

"Gran's got to pay the mortgage off," Polly said. Bless Polly, she could see beyond words. She was growing up. Her comment resulted in more vacant stares at Lydia.

"Are you happy about this?" Ellie asked. "I mean, moving to a retirement flat..."

Like everyone else to whom she had spoken about this situation, Lydia did not want to confess to the doubts, the grief and the sleepless nights the plan had engendered. "Of course I am."

"Oh, well," said Kate, not giving away anything but her disinterest, "I suppose you want to do it."

"I'm sure we all wish you luck," Ellie said. She cleared her throat. "Can I tell my news now?"

That had got Mum out of the way, Lydia reflected. Now for the real people, the younger people, the ones who still 'had a life'.

There was a murmur of agreement rippling around the table. Lydia noticed Ellie's hand was shaking. She wondered why this could be. She had made similar announcements before, perhaps not in the celebratory setting of a family meal, but many 'this is the one' statements, which subsequently all proved to be not about 'the one'.

Ellie took a gulp of wine. "I've met someone," she said.

Nobody voiced the thought, 'Again?' But it hovered over the gathering.

"Tell us," Polly said.

"How lovely." Lydia made an effort. "Yes, tell us all about him."

Ellie took a deep breath. Her cheeks were two spots of pink. Lydia could not understand what her anxiety was. A rapid list of reasons flicked through her mind. Old? Young? Divorced? Foreign? Disabled? Not yet divorced?

"It's not a him, it's a her."

A stunned silence hit the room.

Dan summed it up, a gleam in his eye, and, Lydia surmised, a fantasy in his mind. "You mean, you're a lesbian?"

"Good grief," said Kate, "I never thought of that. When you hinted at someone new, I went through a list in my mind. Was he foreign, or old or perhaps very fat or something? I never thought of a woman."

Beads of perspiration were breaking out on Ellie's brow.

"What's her name?" Polly said.

"Rosie. She's a dance teacher. I met her at the dance studio I go to."

Kate leaned forward. "What does she look like?"

"Very attractive."

"Older? Younger than you?" Kate asked.

"Younger. By two years."

Now everyone noticed that Lydia had not

44

contributed to the questions. They were all looking at her. She knew she looked less than delighted. She was much less than delighted, she was thoroughly disturbed.

"Mum?" Ellie was frowning.

"I'm sorry, Ellie, but have you thought this through?"

"Thought?" Ellie was annoyed. "This is not a head decision. This comes from the heart."

"That's what I mean. You need to think about these things. I am surprised at this choice."

"It's not a choice. It's who I am."

"Then why has it taken you so long to find out who you are?" Lydia knew her voice sounded sharp, but it was not as sharp as her thinking. Ellie, lovely though she was, could be so impulsive.

"Why not?"

"You haven't a clue what you're letting yourself in for…"

"Mum!" Ellie protested.

"Are you desperate not to be on your own, or something? Why have you settled for this? How do you expect me to take this - this bizarre notion seriously, when I've watched you for years go from man to man and always end up with a crisis?"

Nick moved. He threw down his cutlery and his napkin. He jumped to his feet and shoved his chair backwards from the table. He glared at Lydia.

"You bloody bigot," he snarled and left the room. The language made her gasp as did the assumption behind it.

"I'm not a bigot," she protested, close to tears.

Polly leaned back in her chair, placing her knife and fork carefully on her plate. "I'm not eating any more," she said. She turned to Lydia. "I don't know how you can sit there like that after you've upset Ellie so."

"Shush, Polly. It doesn't matter," Ellie said, close to tears herself.

"But it does," Polly, too, was tearful. Now she addressed Lydia. "I can't sit here with you after you've said that. We have lessons at school about not being prejudiced against gays."

"Polly, I'm not prejudiced," Lydia began.

Polly rose, gave Ellie a hug and quietly departed.

Lydia began to tremble. Kate and Dan, when she at last dared to look at them, allowed grim smiles. Kate reached out to Ellie across the table.

"Ellie, I'm so sorry. I didn't know it would be like this. I really didn't. You should have told me. I wouldn't have organised this."

"No. I know. Neither did I. I'm sorry too, that all your efforts have been for nothing. I thought, Mum, you might be a bit negative, embarrassed, even, but not like this, not react like this."

Ellie was sitting opposite Lydia, well-placed for confrontation. They glared at each other. Lydia could not understand why they did not ask her for her reasons.

"It's not your fault, Mum."

"No, it certainly is not." The words were out before she heard what Ellie meant.

"No, Mum. I'm not going to give you credit for my total and utter happiness, if that's what you think. What I was going to say was that it is your generation that are set in their ways and can't update as things change." Ellie turned to Kate. "Rosie says it's mostly the older generation who are so prejudiced against us."

Dan had resumed his meal as though he was no part of this family.

"You think you are trying to change my mind, don't you?" Lydia said. "Let me…"

"Yes," said Ellie, the beautiful, golden Ellie, "I'm trying to clear up a couple of outdated attitudes that you are hanging on to. Sex seems to be a problem with your age group. It's sad for me to realise that you had two children and two marriages and you don't understand the power, the loveliness, of sex."

Wrong, wrong, wrong! Lydia wanted to shout. Who was prejudiced now?

She stood up, rucking the tablecloth as she did so. She was shaky, sure that her knees were going to give way. "I think I'll go home. You don't want to listen to me."

"I don't have a car now, Lydia," Dan said, still eating.

She mopped her mouth on a napkin, pushed her chair out of the way. She stumbled out of the room. Kate followed as she was about to reach for her fur fabric coat.

"Don't go like this, Mum. You're making a fuss about nothing."

"Nothing? If you let me explain…"

"Well, what a pity," Kate hissed, her face close to Lydia's, "what a pity you didn't make a fuss about my life instead of being so keen for me to marry that redundant creep in there." She returned to the dining room.

Lydia was abandoned in the hall, disorientated. Kate had acknowledged difficulty in her marriage and, with regard to Ellie's announcement, no one would allow her to speak. She sank onto the stairs, sitting there, not sure what to do, whether to leave or return to the dining room and to try again.

Kate, Dan, and Ellie had been left silenced in the dining room until Kate went back in there and burst into tears. Lydia could hear her. "I would never have expected this," she sobbed.

"We shouldn't be surprised," Ellie said. "Our parents' generation have what we think of as outdated ideas about a lot of stuff. This is only one of them."

"Don't make excuses for her, Ellie." Kate raised her voice, intending to be heard beyond the dining room. "She was unkind, really."

"She thinks I'm so bad, it's justified. She thinks that insults are not as bad as my – my behaviour."

"Doesn't she, don't all her friends, talk about things? Don't they watch television? Read the newspapers? Don't they have sons and daughters, grandsons and grand-daughters who get up to things they didn't when they were younger? Doesn't she know about same-sex marriage?"

"She's just a bitter old bat because she didn't have fun," Dan said.

"Don't you start!" That was Kate.

"Shush!" Ellie said.

"No, I won't shush. She's not his mother. We've only got one mother, Ellie, and she's turned on us. You, especially. Didn't you think she might react like that?"

"I thought she'd be low key about it, but not, not like this. We're her daughters."

"Doesn't she love us?"

"Believe me, she thinks that's what she's doing. I don't know why she thinks it's wrong but she does and she wants it right."

"You know," Dan said and his slow deliberate way of speaking was even more slow and deliberate, "we could find ourselves being just the same towards Nick or Polly or both in ten or twenty years' time, about some other issue."

"That's true." Ellie said.

"I'll never," Kate said, "never, ever, treat my children with such hatred as she has treated you, Ellie."

"I didn't see any hatred," said Dan.

"Oh, be quiet, you," Kate said to him.

"It remains to be seen. Do you really think that was hatred?" Ellie was determined to be understanding and Kate would not cope with that.

"She should at least show a bit of tolerance," Kate said.

"Tolerance? How patronising! What I need is acceptance. Total acceptance."

Me too, thought Lydia, trying to shift her position on the stairs.

"Look," came Ellie's more upbeat tone, "I think what I need is a nice coffee. Shall I go and make it? Let's all go back into the sitting room."

"I'll make it," Dan volunteered. "I'll clear this lot too. You go into the sitting room."

Dan emerged into the hall, laden with a precarious pile of plates of uneaten food.

"You go back in," he said to Lydia as Kate and Ellie slipped past her.

"I think I ought to go back home. Will you call a taxi for me?"

"If you insist. But I think you shouldn't let yourself be put off by them." He took his burden to the kitchen before returning to Lydia still on the stairs.

"Come on," he said, linking his arm with her

unwilling one, "get back in there, Lydia, into the sitting room. Kate loves a row. Don't give her the excuse for one." He tugged her arm and she rose to her feet. She had a conviction that she could be ammunition for his own conflict, with her daughter. Ignoring her, Kate and Ellie returned to the sitting room. Dan pushed open the door for Lydia to edge her way in.

Ellie was stretched out on the sofa, her long legs curled up on it, her feet bare and her shoes on the floor.

"I wish you hadn't done this, Ellie," Kate, standing, was saying to her sister.

"Done what?"

"This. Gone – gone gay. You know."

Ellie smiled a soft smile. "It's not a question of doing, it's a question of being. Are you having a problem with it?" She glanced up when she saw Lydia by the door.

"I haven't gone home," Lydia said, addressing Kate. "You said not to go like this, so I haven't. I want to explain."

Kate turned away from Lydia.

"Good," Ellie said. "It isn't easy for me, you know. And, Kate, it isn't easy for Mum, either."

"I want to explain," Lydia said again, sinking into the chair she usually occupied.

"It's not easy for me," Kate said, speaking over Lydia's words. "You aren't the person I thought you were."

"And do you not like the new Ellie?"

"Give me time. What did you say her name was, this woman?"

"Rosie."

"Tell me about Rosie."

Ellie's face lit up. "Rosie is truly wonderful. She's a lovely person. You won't be able to help liking her."

"Who does the cooking?" Kate said.

A roar of laughter escaped Ellie. She threw herself back on the sofa, bouncing with amusement. Watching, Lydia saw that Kate was discomfited by what she saw as an innocuous question causing a rumpus.

Ellie sat up. "I know what you're asking. You want to know who is the man, don't you? Well, it's not like that."

The door opened slowly and Polly reappeared.

"I'm cross with you, Gran."

"Yes, I know. I want to explain, Polly."

"What's funny?" Polly addressed Ellie.

"Nothing's funny," Lydia said. "There's been a misunderstanding and I want to explain but nobody is listening." She wrestled her way out of the chair. "I think I'll go home after all. Never mind about a taxi, Dan. I'll walk."

"You can't do that. It's raining. It's Sunday. There aren't many buses."

"Can't I?" This was one of many occasions on which she wished she could make a dignified exit into a waiting car. She had never learned to drive. She had always relied on a husband.

"You two," she addressed Ellie and Kate, aware that she was not acting the gentle, caring mother for once, "you are preventing me speaking. When I think how you both were allowed to express your opinions about my relationship with Peter, your opinions about him, it makes my blood boil that you won't listen to *me* now. The trouble you caused, especially you, Ellie, was unbelievable and out of all proportion to your complaint, to the situation."

51

She paused for breath, her chest heaving.

"Calm down, Mum." That was Kate. "You'll make yourself ill."

"*I'll* make myself ill? What has made me ill before now has been your total lack of understanding of what I was going through after Peter died. You abandoned me---."

"You abandoned me!" Ellie interrupted.

"Not an ounce of sympathy from either of you," Lydia went on. "I understood that you thought *I'd* abandoned *you* when I left your father. One of these days, I'll tell you the nasty truth about him, the violence, the rages, the threats, and yes, the rapes."

She stopped, her breath rasping, the only sound in the otherwise stunned silence. She saw the expression of horror on Polly's face.

She pushed her way past Dan, who was coming in with a tray of coffee cups. She shrugged herself untidily into her fur coat and hurried out of the front door.

Head held high, and with long, angry strides, she forged her way down the road, away from number forty-seven. Once she turned the corner of Alexandra Street, she wilted, slowed her pace. Her shoulders drooped, she trembled.

She'd done it now, the one thing she'd always vowed she would never do, tell them something of the truth about their father. Even in the throes of Ellie's tantrums and insults aimed at Peter and against the changes foisted on the girls, she had resisted that. Now she had burned her boats. They would never forgive her.

It had been a shock, Ellie's announcement. Ellie, lovely, gentle Ellie, her personality so feminine, so attractive, why on earth had she chosen that path? How had it happened? Ellie had claimed that this was who she was. "What shall I do?" Lydia asked herself as she aimed for the bus stop. "Why won't they let me explain?" She wanted to be at home. There was the bus stop, just yards ahead if only she could reach it. What had caused Ellie to turn out like this, always changing partners, becoming involved with married men, much younger men, older men, always experimenting? Now she was with a woman. Was it leaving the girls' father when Ellie was only twelve that had distorted her understanding of relationships? Perhaps she should have explained to both of them why she had divorced him, her fears that, when he exploded, they too might have been physically hurt. Should she have not protected them from the truth? She didn't know the answers.

A weakness was washing over her. Her brain was swimming. She leaned against the lamp post on which the sign for the bus stop was fixed. She felt unwell. There was a pain in her chest. She was going to die. She had left them all, Polly as well, with this ill-humour which even now she could not abandon. In her preoccupations, she had not seen the bus draw up. She startled. Passengers alighted. With relief she noted that there were people around. She reached out blindly for the rail to haul herself onto the bus. There was hardly enough strength in her to lift her bus pass to the driver.

"You all right, love?" It was the friendly driver again, not smiling, this time, but frowning in concern.

"I've got pains," Lydia murmured.

Another passenger, seeing what was happening, leaped forward and guided Lydia to the nearest seat. She sank onto it, not forgetting to grasp her handbag tightly.

It contained cash, cash she had intended for Nick and Polly, for it was not their fault their father had been made redundant. Then she recalled Nick calling her a bigot and swearing at her. There had been a lack of understanding on their part. If only they had asked her, allowed her to explain her misgivings. Please God, let her have time to put it all right, to tell them how much she loved them.

The driver phoned for an ambulance. She had locked her cab and was beside Lydia.

"How'd you feel, love?"

"Scared. Pains. In my chest."

"Can you breathe slowly, long, deep breaths?"

Lydia obediently breathed with long, deep breaths.

"Any the other pains? In your arm, for instance?"

Lydia shook her head. Wasn't it enough to have pains in her chest?

"You'll be okay," the driver said. She smiled.

"Will I?" Lydia hoped so. She didn't want to die, not in this frame of mind, not at all. Not yet.

"I think so."

She began to relax. The ambulance arrived. So soon? Was it serious after all? The paramedics helped her to move, supporting her. What a spectacle she must be presenting, a pathetic old woman in a pathetic fur fabric coat.

The paramedics asked questions. She shut her eyes and answered in a mumble. The pain had gone, she sank into a doze where nothing really mattered. On waking she found she was lying on a trolley in the hospital. She was alive. How could she be certain? And why bother? Her hips hurt on the hard surface on which she lay.

She was examined, prodded and questioned.

"Well, Mrs Grover, I'm glad to tell you that there is nothing wrong with you," said the handsome young man at her side, a doctor, presumably.

Lydia forced herself up through the mist. "What?"

"Have you had a shock, or bad news? Or a lot of stress, lately?"

"Yes. Today. Lunchtime. It was unpleasant. There was a-a disagreement. And I'm planning to move."

"All that would explain it. Anxiety. Try to relax, Mrs Grover. You can go home. As soon as you like. We'll give you some tablets to take, to calm you. And make sure you see your GP."

"How do I get home?" she said.

He was about to move away. "How did you get here?"

"Ambulance."

"Then I'm afraid you'll have to phone your family or take a taxi."

Lydia mumbled angrily about the NHS no longer being like it was in her younger days, the youth of the doctor and the fact that no one thought to help her off the trolley, which was too high for her to manage with confidence. She staggered from A and E to the hospital entrance where she phoned for a taxi to take her home. It was a quarter past eight. She had no idea where the time had gone since lunch time. At home, she would be left alone to mull over her misery and ruminate on the events of the afternoon and the prospects for the future.

* * *

55

Dark thoughts filled Lydia's nights, thoughts of anger, even revenge, scenarios of confrontation with Ellie and Kate and above all, doubts about the move to Tarascon Court. Neither Kate nor Ellie had shown support or interest in her plans, which had been partly motivated, it must be acknowledged, by sympathy for Kate's financial difficulties. She had always tried to overlook her daughters' attitude to Peter, yet when she voiced her concerns over Ellie embarking on an unconventional lifestyle, she was accused of being a bigot, of being prejudiced. They didn't know, Kate and Ellie, what she knew. She would have to tell them, if she had the chance. As her daughters had grown up, she had protected them far too much.

And then there was Kate's marriage…

Yet, none of these thoughts touched on the most horrifying question of all, a thought given momentum by her feeling ill at the bus-stop and by the idea of moving to Tarascon Court, the fact that, one day, she was going to die. Her biggest fear was that this would happen when she was alone, away from her daughters. It was not in some far distant, fuzzy future, but most likely within a span of time ahead, as short as the duration of her marriage to Peter had been, twenty years or so. This she hardly dared dwell upon. The prospect of the move had made her aware that she was getting older, and getting older ended with dying. When she did dwell on all this, alone in the big house, with no one to call upon, no one at all since Sunday, her terror was unbearable.

After two sleepless nights, she decided she had to do something about these preoccupations, so she visited her GP, before going to the library, which was what she had done after Peter died, and come away with an armful of books on bereavement. Today she was concerned about her own death.

She was able to reserve time at a computer in order to compile a list of books that would enlighten her on the subject of death and dying, even perhaps, diminish her fears. A few were available immediately, others she needed to collect another day. She was standing at the counter, dealing with this, when her name was spoken softly behind her.

"Lydia?"

She turned. Clive Morris was standing there in an overcoat and scarf, a dapper figure, books tucked under his arm.

"Clive. Hello."

"Hello, Lydia. How are you?"

"Oh, I'm fine," she lied.

His expression told her he did not believe it. She saw his eyes taking in the titles of the books she was hugging.

"How's it going?" He must be talking about the sale and purchase, not the turmoil inside her.

"All is going well. I'm hoping to exchange contracts, complete and move in, all on the same day in less than four weeks' time. I'm exhausted with the tension." She stepped away from the counter, having made her requests, so he stepped up to reserve his own choice.

"We all go through it," he said.

"Through what?"

"These doubts."

"About the move? Nobody admits to them though, do they?"

He stepped back from the counter, the assistant all but ignoring him. "It's in the past once you've moved in. You need to get on with the afternoon of life then, you see."

"The afternoon of life? Of my life?" she mused, thinking hers was becoming a wet and dreary afternoon with the prospect of a dark and lonely evening.

He glanced at his watch, concealed under a neat white shirt cuff. "Look," he said, "have you got time for a cup of coffee? Claire's Tea Rooms is two doors away."

They walked together along the pavement to the most popular tea rooms in the town. "I would suggest a drink in the Green Goddess," he said with a nod to the up-market gastro-pub across the road, "but I'm teetotal. Drink problem, you know."

Lydia looked at him properly for the first time, so respectable, so calm and pleasant. Who would have thought he had a problem like that? At this age, though, everyone had a past, lots of past. She had hers, which had been like a dead weight at times. Tarascon Court had precipitated a huge shift in her consciousness.

She and Clive sat down in the window of the pink and blue decorated tearooms.

"They do a really wonderful hot chocolate here. Would you like one? My treat. You look as though you need some indulgence. You appear rather tired."

She smiled. After two days and nights of self punishing thoughts, a hot chocolate drink would be heaven. "Thank you. Yes, I am tired. I collapsed on Sunday. On the bus. I was taken to hospital. I thought I was having a heart attack. They said it was just stress, gave me some tablets and told me to go to my GP."

"And have you? Been to your GP?"

"Yes, just now. I was too stunned for a day or so. I

thought I was going to die. It wasn't a heart attack, though. Stress. I couldn't believe it."

"Is this about the move?"

"Partly. I had a row with my two daughters on Sunday."

"You can be more independent when you move. You won't need to rely on them so much."

More independent? She thought she was hardly dependent on them now, certainly not to the extent that Veronica was dependent on Ashton. If only! "I would like their goodwill, their approval. They still disapprove of my second marriage. It's nearly five years since my husband died."

The hot chocolate arrived, comfort topped with whipped cream. She couldn't help a smile.

"A not uncommon story," he said.

She was talking too much. There was a need in her to make up for the self-imposed isolation in which she had been since Peter's death. Her living had been suspended, as though he was worth more than even the five years she had since given him.

"I'm coming to choir tomorrow," she said, more as a promise to herself than anything. "What with the weather and moving, I've missed two weeks."

"Difficult, this time of the year," Clive said. "You shouldn't worry, you know. You'll fit in well at Tarascon Court. On our corridor there are some really nice people. Cathy, at number thirty, you'll get on with her. When she's at home. She's got five sisters and three children so she's always away, spending time with one or the other of them. And Tara, in Ireland at the moment. She's next door to you, at twenty-seven. And Sue the manager, she's great."

"The thing is," she burst out, "the money, the difference

in the sale and purchase prices, is going to become a barrier between us, between me and my daughters. One of the reasons I first thought of moving to Tarascon Court was I wanted to help Kate's financial problems. But it's more difficult than I thought it might be." Hugging the house because it had been Peter's now suggested selfishness and sentimentality.

"Most people," Clive said after a pause, "who live at Tarascon Court, would recognise that. You haven't been selected as a particularly bad mother."

Lydia was beginning to see clearly, Kate's and Ellie's position. Neither of them would ask for, nor accept money, from her because of the disagreement about Peter. She herself would find it difficult to offer money in case it was refused. Trying to breach either position would escalate the antipathy between them. Nobody in the equation wanted to appear to be buying or selling affection, loyalty. And that was without taking Dan's spending habits into consideration.

"I need to get a life," she said, thinking of Polly's quip.

"You will. Your own life. A life that you choose, not what you think you ought to have. I wish I'd made the move sooner. I find I'm doing things I always thought I'd never have time for."

"Such as? Apart from the choir?"

"Theatre, films, the University of the Third Age, the bowls club. There's lots to do."

"Bingo in the lounge at Tarascon Court?"

"Darts, actually." He laughed. "I have time. No worries, you see, about a lot of bricks and mortar. Not a lot of housework, or gardening. Oh, it's a great life. I have time for people at last."

Clive made his life sound attractive. But then there was the problem of death. Once at home, she settled down, on the sofa in her snug, to her studies, a glass of wine at her elbow and a cheese sandwich for lunch. She remained there until the light began to fade, reluctant to pursue the subject alone in the dark. She turned to television and trivia, with a small satisfaction that she was finally facing that which she had avoided for so long, even in the face of Peter's example.

* * *

A few days later, the door bell ringing at a quarter to eight in the evening, sent her heart thumping. She crept across the hall. Only Kate, in recent weeks, had called at such a time. She hardly dared hope that her daughter had come to heal the breach between them.

When she reached the door, Lydia called out, "Who is it?"

"Polly," came the reply.

"Polly? On your own?"

" 'Course not. Mum's with me."

Lydia opened the door. Under the porch light stood an unsmiling Kate with Polly, who was more relaxed.

"Hello, dears. This is a lovely surprise. I'm really pleased to see you." Lydia wrapped her arms around each of them. Kate's resistance could not be mistaken. Neither Kate nor Polly spoke as Lydia led them to the snug.

"I've come to sort things out," Kate said, tossing her coat over a chair and sinking onto the sofa. Polly slipped down beside her, nudging under her mother's arm as though seeking shelter.

"I'm glad." Lydia spoke slowly. "I have many things on my mind. On a practical level, I have to clear this house. I can't take everything with me. There are things I want you to have before I move."

"Gran took me to see her new flat last Saturday. It's quite small." Polly was bouncing and wriggling in her unease.

"Have you not told your Mum?"

"You said not to," Polly said.

"Only until the lunch and until I'd told you all."

Kate's face was like thunder. "No, she didn't tell me. I didn't know."

Lydia glanced from her daughter to her grand-daughter. "I'm sorry about that. It wasn't my intention to deceive you. I can arrange to take you, too, if you like, Kate. I could do with some advice on top of Polly's."

Kate was not be softened. "You and I need to talk," she said. "Is there something you can give Polly to do? I need to concentrate."

"Why don't you," Lydia addressed Polly, "why don't you roam around and choose one or two things, dear? Ornaments, pictures, lamps, cushions. You know, the sort of thing you can carry home."

"Can I really?" Polly jumped to her feet and darted out to the hall.

"Put the lights on. We don't want any accidents," Lydia called after her.

Now they were left together, she and Kate, facing each other across the room. The soft golden light from the lamps, the cosy warm atmosphere were the opposite of what Lydia could read on Kate's face.

"I don't like the idea of you and Polly having secrets from me. But that's not what I came to discuss."

"No?" Lydia's hopes did a dive. She feared the pains returning. "I must say one thing about that, Kate. I do think Nick should apologise to me. I am not a bigot. And there was no reason to swear at me. Why you didn't correct him there and then, I cannot understand." She drew a deep breath and dived in to the subject they both feared having to face. "The whole episode was the result of a total misunderstanding, anyway."

"Your misunderstanding, Mum. You haven't updated your ideas yet to keep up with the rest of the population."

Leaning back in her chair, determined not to be provoked, Lydia tried to meet Kate halfway.

"I am well aware that I was brought up to function in a world that doesn't exist any more and that you expect less of me then you do of your peers. But then, so were you. None of my generation ever knew how the world would change for your generation any more than my mother could predict my adult world."

The olive branch was rejected.

"You've upset Ellie, terribly."

"Is she all right? Not ill or anything?"

"I told you. She's extremely upset. You've taken all the joy out of her life."

"So easily?"

"Oh, there are times when I hate you, Mum. She feels you've turned against her. You don't agree with her being gay and that's her life. Not yours."

"You're a bit too anxious to think badly of me." Lydia paused. She didn't want to make excuses, to explain herself. That was not the way to persuade Kate to see her point of view.

Kate threw herself back in the sofa, "Oh!" she groaned spreading her palms as if to say "See?"

"Is it surprising," Lydia began, "after the way Ellie's lurched from man to man for years, not to mention more than one at a time, on occasions? You can't blame me for thinking she might be now going from woman to woman, can you? I haven't turned against her at all."

"Yes, you have, you're cruel. And, fancy saying that about rape in front of Polly. Not that I believe a word of it, anyway. As for the rest of your diatribe, everything goes back to Peter, doesn't it? You can't forget it and you can't forgive us."

"I'm of the opinion it is you two who can't forgive me."

"Here we go again."

"Listen, Kate." Lydia leaned forward to appeal to her daughter. "If you knew what I know, if you'd not been so negative about Peter –."

"Oh, that's it, is it? Revenge. Now Ellie knows how it feels, does she? She really played you up, didn't she, you and your precious Peter? Everything goes back to that bore."

"Honestly, Kate, you are so insulting. You don't need to be." Lydia leaned back in her chair, defeated. She was close to tears but didn't want to give Kate the satisfaction of seeing that.

"You're just prejudiced. And bitter."

"Kate, please, I'm not."

"You're anti-gay and too proud to admit it."

"I'm not…"

Her lips pressed together, with narrowed eyes, Kate gazed into the distance refusing to focus on Lydia.

"It's not like that," Lydia said. "I'm beginning to feel upset."

"So you should."

"I was ill after I left on Sunday. I was taken ill at the bus stop and rushed to hospital. I had chest pains."

Even that Kate resisted. "If you had a heart attack, why are you back home here so soon?"

"I never said it was a heart attack. They said it was stress. You and Ellie, you've got it all wrong. I don't want to argue with you. I'm concerned about you. And your family. I want to help you. Both of you. Let me help you."

"Do you mean money? God, I don't believe you. You're trying to buy me now. Let you help me and be indebted to you for the rest of my life? And after the way you behaved on Sunday? You are the lowest, aren't you?"

Polly appeared in the doorway. Her eyes darted from Lydia to Kate.

"You haven't mended it, have you? Gran is upset."

This sympathy was more than Lydia could manage. Two tears rolled down her cheeks. Polly hurried over to her.

"I know why you're crying, Gran. It's about Ellie, isn't it? You think she shouldn't be gay, don't you?"

Lydia shook her head, loosening more tears. She sniffed and dashed them away with her hand. Perching on the arm of the chair, Polly launched into a little speech she must had been preparing while moving around upstairs.

"It's like war, isn't it? You thought war was okay, didn't you, when you were a girl. Do you still? Because I don't, you see. And hanging. People your age still think it's okay even though we don't do it. But *we* don't think it's right, people our age. You've got to catch up. You've got to update, Gran."

For the first time since Kate and Polly had arrived, Lydia smiled. She almost laughed. The speech was touching. Polly was a clever, thoughtful girl.

"And what, dear Polly, do you think your generation will have to catch up on?"

A pensive expression came over Polly's eager face. She tilted her head. "You mean not understanding people? I think it would be old people. We don't like older people. We say they're a drain on the economy and stuff like that."

One glance at Kate's stony face, one ironic glance and Lydia burst out laughing. "So long," she said, breathless with amusement, "so long as you update in time for your own old age."

Still Kate failed to see the joke. "Come on, Polly. Get your coat on. We're going." Her glance fell on a figurine Polly was clasping close to her chest. "What's that?"

"It's Lladro. A shepherdess. I've always liked it."

"Put it down," Kate said.

"But, Gran said –."

"Put it down. Anywhere. Come on. We're going home."

Polly obeyed, tossing the shepherdess into Lydia's lap. She followed Kate out of the room, while struggling into her coat. Kate grasped her by the elbow and propelled her across the hall to the front door.

Lydia hurried after them. "Kate, Kate, listen. There's something I have to tell you. Peter had a –."

"Don't keep bringing him into it."

"If only you'd listen, you and Ellie."

"Stay away from her. She doesn't want anything to do with you." Kate wrenched open the front door, pushing Polly ahead of her. Before the door slammed, Lydia caught sight of Polly's strained face peering back over her shoulder.

* * *

After some wet, cold days, which included a few flurries of snow, Polly was again on Lydia's doorstep.

Lydia was pleased to see her. "On your own, dear?"

"Yes. I've come for the shepherdess."

"Does Mum know you're here? Make sure you tell her." She led Polly to the snug. They passed through the hall, Polly registering the chaos, the boxes and cases everywhere. She was bound to be upset. This house had been a landmark in her childhood, her grandmother's house, she had spent many a sleepover here and it was about to be taken away from them both forever.

Polly threw her coat over a chair. "It's all a muddle, isn't it?"

"Yes. It's necessary though. I have to sort stuff."

"I meant the, you know, disagreement."

"Yes, that too. That most of all," Lydia said, patting a space beside her on the sofa. "I'm sorry, Polly, but the shepherdess has gone with the rest of the Lladro and is packed safely in a box. I'll come over, in a taxi, one evening before I move. I'll bring it, along with some things I want everyone else to have, Nick included."

"He swore at you."

"That was a terrible day."

"I think it's sad you moving. Are you really going to do it?"

"I think it's wise."

Polly's eyes roamed around the room, noticing the changes.

"Yes, the pictures have gone, the willow pattern is packed. There are more boxes over there, waiting to be filled, Polly. It's upsetting, isn't it?"

"Mum says you don't mean it. The move. She says you won't do it. Because of Peter."

"I will and I am."

"When are you going to do it?"

"A week next Monday."

"Why did you say moving is wise?"

"I've had to admit that the house is too much for me. And it's too lonely."

"The flat's nice, isn't it? Why did Mum say you keep bringing Peter into it? Why didn't she like him?"

"I'll tell you," Lydia said, rising awkwardly from the low sofa. She went through to the kitchen, to return carrying a biscuit tin and a glass of lemonade. The lemonade she placed on the low table by Polly. She removed the lid of the biscuit tin and offered it to Polly.

"Have a biscuit, Polly."

Polly took two biscuits.

"Peter," she said, "I'd love to tell you about him. Even now Kate and Ellie don't like the mention of him. To understand, just imagine if your Mum left your Dad and made her life with someone else, what would you think?"

"I'd be cross with Mum, especially if she took me away from my home."

"Exactly. Kate and Ellie are cross with me."

"Still?"

Lydia lifted her palms with a shrug. "It seems so. He was a lovely man. So thoughtful and caring." She smiled.

Polly watched her, curious. "He tried so hard to be accepted by them. Of course, Ellie was living here after Peter and I got together. Her room was the one you sleep in when you come for the night."

"Why did you leave my Grandad to be with him? Where did you meet him?"

"I met him at work. I was in an estate agents'. He came in. I didn't realise at first that he owned the whole company."

"Was it falling in love at first sight?"

"I suppose so."

Polly sighed. "And my Grandad? I never knew him."

"He was a bad-tempered creature. He was unkind, he frightened my girls. They seem to have forgotten that. When I met Peter, it was like instant recognition. I'd never felt anything like it before."

Polly watched her grandmother's face. "You look happy when you talk about him." She glanced away from Lydia, then drew her eyes back in a short, coy glance, "Did you love him?"

"Oh, so much, Polly. I would wish that much happiness for you."

They both sat still for a few moments. "I wish Mum and Dad could be like that."

"Are they going through a bad patch?"

Polly nodded. "They argue a lot. When I said I didn't like it, Mum said it was just a phase. Phases are short, aren't they? This one is going on for a long time."

"I'm not saying there weren't problems for me and Peter. My girls, they played up. Life, however happy, is never plain sailing."

Polly's thoughts seemed to be elsewhere now. "I want to tell you something, Gran. Don't laugh at me.

Do you remember that day, the day you took me to see the new flat?"

"Of course I do."

"And Mr Hornby was in the other lady's flat, his mother's flat. And he kissed his mother good-bye. Do you remember?"

"Yes. I do."

Polly looked down. Two spots of high colour rose rapidly to her cheeks. "Am I silly, because I kept thinking of that and wishing it was me he'd kissed."

Lydia put an arm across her shoulders. Polly continued to focus her gaze towards the floor.

"No, of course not, Polly. That sort of thing happens. Have you been worrying about that?"

"No, not that. There's worse. You see, in maths, with Mr Hornby right close to me, I kept thinking of that because my homework was covered with kisses, well, not kisses. They were crosses for wrong calculations. He said something to me and I didn't hear properly. He said, 'Come on, Pauline, concentrate. You know this. What do I do next?' And I wanted to say, 'Kiss me', and I don't know if I said it or just thought it. It was awful. I burst into tears and ran out of the room." And she burst into tears again.

"Oh, Polly. I'm sure you didn't say it."

"Jez says I didn't say anything."

Jez? Oh yes, the boy in her class, Polly's protector. "Did you tell him what you thought you said?"

"No way!"

"Then you can be sure you didn't say it."

"Gran, what's rape?"

"Being forced to have sex."

Polly looked puzzled. "That doesn't sound very romantic. Mum says sex is dangerous."

"Yes, it can be."

Polly pondered briefly. "Like nuclear power?" she said. "Nuclear power is useful, isn't it? But it can be dangerous."

"Yes, I suppose so." Lydia threw her head back and laughed heartily, disturbing the pile of books stacked at her feet, next to the sofa. Polly tucked them back into a tidy pile, looking to see what they were. Lydia saw a strange expression pass over the girl's face.

"I've got to go home," Polly said. She snatched her coat before rushing across the hall to the front door. In a kind of frenzy, she undid the bolts, turned the key, slipped through a narrow opening. The door slammed and Polly was gone.

Lydia looked at the pile of books, registering the titles as Polly might have seen them. Containing the words 'death' and 'dying', they could have been crime novels, except that some of the authors were doctors.

Over the week-end, Polly phoned. "I needn't worry now about Mr Hornby thinking I'm a tart."

"Oh, good," Lydia said, amused.

"He's left our school, the traitor. I'll never get my maths GCSE now. We've got Mrs Watson back. He's gone to Mum's school, Mr Hornby, to the little kids. They won't appreciate him there."

* * *

To avoid the torment of 'last minutes' at the house and the arising of a temptation to change her mind, Lydia planned to make a clean break with the past before the move. She booked a room in the Castle Hotel for Friday, Saturday and Sunday nights.

It was Friday afternoon and the house was still and

empty of all but the items she needed at Tarascon Court. Her bedding was folded, never to be slept in again in the bedroom here. Her clothes, neatly packed in cases and hold-alls waited to be transported to the new home. The electricity, gas, water and the central heating were all switched off, windows closed and locked. All that remained to be done was to pack her small case for the Castle Hotel.

In the bathroom, items were assembled on a glass shelf waiting to be popped into her capacious toilet bag, its size yet another trivial reminder of encroaching age. Necessities proliferated as she grew older. Pantyliners, just in case, special toothpaste to stop the ache caused by hot drinks on a cold day, natural skin care preparations for a drying skin, the list could be endless in a year or two. She laughed grimly as she lifted the much-depleted bottle of scent that Peter had given her and which Kate found so objectionable. Whether it was her nervous fingers or an influence more subtle than that, she would never know. The bottle slipped from her grasp to smash on the tiled floor.

For the last time in nearly a quarter of a century, Lydia, as the owner of the house, unlocked, drew back the bolts and opened the front door. There was a lump in her throat. She stepped over the threshold. In the drive a taxi waited, its engine chugging patiently. All the boxes of gifts for members of the family were loaded into it. Some were small, of shoe box size, others larger, and one, for Kate, was the only one too heavy for Lydia to lift. She'd had to slide it across the hall floor, pushing it with her feet to reach the front door for the taxi driver to lift it down the steps. She had also added, for Kate, the fake fur coat, last worn to the fateful lunch party at her house. That coat seemed out of place in the modest environment of Tarascon Court. A big coat in a small flat! Ridiculous.

Blindly, she pulled the door shut, turned the key in the lock and stepped down to the waiting taxi. She slid into the back seat, dropped the keys into her handbag, clasping a bouquet for Veronica.

"Forty seven Alexandra Street," she instructed the driver.

The evening star shone in a clear turquoise sky, the air was sharp, promising frost. She would remember this, her last real departure from the house. Monday was moving day. All she had to do then was to supervise the removal men. There was not a great deal to supervise, just the beds, the sofa, her table and chairs, the electric cooker and some linen and kitchenware. Her pruning had been rigorous. She had relinquished all unnecessary burdens by moving to Tarascon Court. She would be living simply. Even the goodwill of Kate and Ellie had been foregone. After the recent weeks of resentment, she decided to try to have no expectations of them, to hope no longer for an opportunity to explain. Now she was heading for Kate's home, after which there was to be a short visit to Veronica at Tarascon Court before a week-end of luxury in the town's Castle Hotel.

Polly answered the door at number forty seven. Lydia gazed in astonishment at the girl's appearance. Her hair was scraped back brutally into a ponytail. Her eyebrows had been pencilled in, dark and hard. Her lips were a dark scarlet and round her eyes, her lashes were stiff with mascara, like iron railings. The colour of the lids above them was dark and sinister. Lydia stifled a response.

"Hello, dear. Would you tell Mum I'm here but I haven't come to linger. Just a flying visit."

"She's not home yet," Polly said. "What's this? Who are the flowers for?"

The taxi driver was unloading the boxes, the biggest, with Kate's name on it, first.

"Oh, that's a shame," Lydia said. "They're for Veronica, the flowers." It was a relief, really, that Kate was not there. "That's the dinner set I promised Kate. These boxes are yours, two of them. The Lladro's in this one, and a few other things. Do what you like with them, Polly. Sell them if you want. I'm moving on Monday." That was reckless, but gifts were not supposed to have conditions attached to them.

"Mum's very late," Polly said, ignoring the boxes that were accumulating in the hall. "It's gone six o'clock," she continued. "She's usually home before this."

"Tied up in school. It's half-term next week, isn't it? She's probably got a lot of stuff to catch up on." Lydia leaned forward to kiss Polly on the cheek. "Be good. And remember, subtle is more effective with boys. That applies to make-up as well." And she hurried back to the waiting taxi.

"Tarascon Court, now," she said to the taxi driver, noting that he had remembered to leave her case in the vehicle, earning himself a nice tip. On her way in, she encountered Cathy, of whom Clive had spoken. She seemed younger than Lydia, and friendly, a slender person, dressed casually.

"When are you moving in?" she asked.

Lydia told her it would be Monday.

"Are you looking forward to it?"

"I'll be glad when it's over. I've had so many doubts about doing this. It's still not too late. And you're never sure, are you, that the purchaser can come up with the money, or even doesn't have their own doubts."

"They usually do come up with the money," Cathy said. "There are sanctions if they don't. Your doubts will end when you walk in on Monday. I don't regret coming here. It's a pity it's next week you're moving in. I'm due to visit my sister in London for a few days then, or I'd offer to help you."

"That's kind of you, but I am well-organised. So far. I'm visiting Veronica now."

Cathy wished her the best of luck with the whole process and Lydia made her way up to the fourth floor and Veronica's flat.

Veronica was in a state of agitation. "I'm waiting for Ashton. He's very late. It's half-term next week and he'll be free from now on. I have to go to the hospital Out-patients next week."

"Perhaps there's a lot to catch up on. These are for you, to thank you for your kindness."

"Thank you." Veronica was more concerned with Ashton than appearing grateful for a bunch of flowers. "I'm so glad you're coming to live here," she said as she retreated in her high heels from the front door to her living room. "We all worry about who comes to vacant flats. And I've told everyone you're such a nice lady."

"I'm hope I'm able to live up to that."

Veronica collapsed into the safety of her recliner chair. Lydia registered the hope that this woman was not going to be too clinging once the move had been accomplished. She could see she was the dependent type, missing the comfort and support of a strong husband.

She sat on the other reclining chair, placing her handbag and two books by her feet on the floor. "I've left my case in your hall. Is that all right with you?"

"Your case?"

"Yes, remember, I'm going to the Castle Hotel when I leave you. For three nights. You've been such a help, Veronica, I brought a little gift to say thank you."

"Oh, you shouldn't," was Veronica's predictable reply, belied by her eagerness to see what Lydia was pulling from her bag. "You've already given me the flowers. Where did I put them?"

"Just a token. Speciality shortbread."

"Oh," Veronica clasped her hands above her soft, crêpe-skinned bosom. "I do so love shortbread. Thank you so much." Her eyes lighted on the two books Lydia had brought with her. "Are you going to spend the weekend reading?"

"I am. I'm indulging in all my passions. Food, luxury, reading, you know."

"What are you reading?" The question was one of politeness.

"Library books," Lydia said as she passed the books to her.

Veronica gasped. "Lydia! Are they about what I think they are?"

"Death?" The word held less fear for Lydia now.

Veronica shuddered. "Oh, how morbid. How can you be alone and read about death and dying. So morbid, Lydia, so morbid."

"Not if you understand, think about it and face up to it," said Lydia whose recent insights had made her bolder than she had been. "We are all going to do it one day."

"Oh, don't." Veronica shuddered again.

Lydia was glad of this reaction. Nothing would prevent Veronica being demanding more than the prospect of talking about death. Or the other taboo subject.

Now Veronica, as she made tea and arranged biscuits on a plate, was even more agitated. Lydia knew she should have put the books in her bag and tucked the shortbread under her arm or remembered to pack them in her case. There had been so much to think about as she prepared to leave the house. The leaving had been like, well, a bereavement, the end of something big in her life, big and familiar.

The doorbell rang and Veronica, all nerves, clattered plates and saucers on a tray.

"Ashton!" She turned to Lydia. "He's so late. I do hope nothing is wrong."

She tottered to the entry phone. "Oh, Ashie, at last. Where have you been?" She pressed the button then waited for him by her open front door. Lydia could see the yellow sports car, Ashton Hornby's trademark, down in the car park.

"Oh, Ashie!" Veronica said again throwing her arms around him as he stepped into the flat. "Where have you been? Ashie!" Her tone changed. "You've been drinking, haven't you?"

"Yes, Mum. I'm a big boy now, married, divorced, father of one, professional man, it's allowed. Half-term next week. I claimed my reward, that's all."

Over Veronica's shoulder he saw Lydia.

"Hello, Ashton," Lydia said.

"Hello, there." His face was flushed, his eyes, that intense blue, were bright. He was good-looking in a boyish way.

"Lydia moves in here on Monday," Veronica said.

"I've slept in my house for the last time," Lydia said. "I'll be in the hotel until Monday morning. Then I shall go over to the house to let the removal men in. There's not much to move now."

He sat down on the stool next to her chair. "That must have been very difficult for you."

"It was. But the worst is over."

"What about handing over the keys?" he said.

"You do understand, don't you?" she said, adding with a laugh, "I shall shut my eyes."

"She's only reading about dying," Veronica said, tottering in with a full teapot. Lydia and Ashton watched her with attention.

The teapot safely delivered, Ashton turned his blue gaze onto Lydia again. "Brave lady," he said.

"Unnecessary," said Veronica through pursed lips.

Lydia and Ashton smiled.

Tea was poured, there was a lot of small talk, then Ashton rose, having satisfied himself that his mother had no immediate needs, only the hospital appointments next week, he prepared to leave.

"Don't forget," he said to Lydia, "any help you need with the move, lifting and so on, don't hesitate to ask. I won't be far."

When he had gone Veronica came bustling back from the front door.

"I am so glad he ditched that bitch," she said unexpectedly. Lydia guessed she was referring to Ashton's ex-wife. "She was so jealous of my relationship with him."

"He hasn't remarried?"

"No. And I hope he never does."

Later, as Lydia was emerging from the lift, Clive

78

came in through the main door in the entrance hall. A taxi was coming to take her to the hotel.

"Lydia! Are you moving in soon?"

"On Monday. I've shut up the house and I'm going to a hotel for the week-end. A kind of limbo."

"A comfortable one. I've been to the most interesting talk."

"I'm waiting for my taxi. Where was the talk?"

"In the church hall. Round the corner. About ageing, you know, old age. It was wonderful."

She laughed, doubtfully, her eyes were watching for her taxi.

"No, really. The speaker was a woman, eighty if she was a day. She began by saying, *This problem of an ageing population… There isn't one!*' That made everyone sit up, I can tell you. It was the first of a series of talks called '*The Wise Side of Life*'. You should come next week."

"The Wise Side of Life?"

Clive was an eager talker. The taxi seemed a long time arriving. Lydia stood her trolley-case upright and rested her hand on the handle.

"Yes, she said we have these extra years. Why fill them with more of the same? She was so – so *challenging*. You know? She said, '*give up striving and try just being*'. I've got to think about that. Not that I strive an awful lot these days. Not the energy I had when I was younger. So you've shut up your house?"

She swallowed. "I feel frightened when I think of what I've done. I hope I don't live to regret it."

"Just live. Just be. Try just being, like the woman said." He smiled, adding, "Have a comfortable weekend. Here's your taxi. Good luck with the move." And he headed for the lift.

79

Lydia left Tarascon Court for the Castle Hotel in a taxi.

* * *

The hotel receptionist was making an effort to hide her impatience. Lydia fumbled in her handbag for the details of the booking. Take a deep breath, she told herself, stand up straight, as Kate had once told her, pull your shoulders back, take that frown off your face, then people won't think you are a dithery old lady.

She had to acknowledge she was a dithery old lady. The keys of the house were the cause of her dithering. Her concentration had been broken by a sharp stab of fear at the sight of them. They would be relinquished on Monday morning.

"I'm so sorry," she apologised to the young woman. "My brain is fuddled with moving house. It's really unnerving having no home, even if it is for only three nights."

She found the document she needed, received the key to her room and took the lift to the first floor. The room was just what she hoped it would be, muted colours, big windows with voile curtains, a view of the hills across the river and a big double bed. She locked the door, flung her coat over a chair, kicked off her shoes and lay down on the bed. With the pillows re-arranged, she could lean back and relax, knowing there was nothing she needed to do, either for herself or for anyone else. Only Veronica, and Clive knew exactly where she was.

Her body grew heavy, her breathing deep and slow. This was freedom, peace, total freedom, total peace. At this moment, all she had in the world that was of any real importance, was in this room, the contents of which, with the exception of her small trolley-case and her handbag, did not belong to her. In the case was a change of clothes, in her handbag were all the worldly goods she needed, the keys to the house, her cheque book, her diary with phone numbers, her birth and marriage certificates and Peter's death certificate, her debit and credit cards, passport and a copy of her will. She had also brought a small packet of painkillers, just in case. This was travelling light, living light. Only now were the responsibilities of the house, the drain of the duties that went with it, becoming apparent to her. When he was ill, Peter had mentioned that it should be sold. She had protested and her words at that time she had honoured until now.

This evening, all the doubts, all the anxieties were suspended. She sat up on the bed, hugging her knees. Through the voile curtains she could see the river. Beyond were the hills, topped with winter skeletons of beech trees, like pencil drawings against the sunset. A strange exhilaration caught her, lifting her high and making her sharply aware of the relative unimportance of so much in life except the glorious fact of being alive, alert and able to appreciate the vibrancy of living.

She would remember this moment, the sunset moment, for the rest of her life, how secure she was despite being alone, with no tangible security and nothing certain. For three days she would be living free of trappings. That was how her life at Tarascon Court could be, living with fewer trappings.

Of course, there would be a great deal of money going into her bank account on Monday. Yet money, in this frame of mind, was merely theoretical, a myth, a convention that could all disappear at the stroke of someone's pen.

The sun had set. Only a fading red stain remained to silhouette the beech trees. From her case she drew out a long black skirt and plain black top to wear for dinner. She made her way downstairs to the dining room. It was past eight o'clock.

Remaining in this pleasing calm mood, she enjoyed a meal of poached salmon, fresh vegetables, fresh fruit dessert and a glass of wine. Peter seemed close to her.

On returning to her room, she watched a tedious television programme before picking up her books on death and dying. She was becoming less afraid of dying, trying to see it's more as a peak of her life than as a brutal end to it, a change of attitude she fought despite herself. Before deciding to sleep, she made herself a hot chocolate drink, reminding her of Clive at Claire's Tea Rooms, and she checked her phone. There was a message from Kate, to thank her, Lydia naïvely thought, for the dinner set in the box. She laughed when she had listened to it. Poor Kate, poor confused Kate, she had been drinking before she made that call. Was she, Lydia, her mother, such an ogre that her daughter could not face her sober?

"I know what you're doing, you're trying to turn Polly against me because I turned against you when you went off with that gargoyle, Peter."

Poor, unhappy Kate. In the after effects of the sunset moment, Lydia knew what would be best for her daughter. But for the same reason, she saw clearly that she must never venture to put it into words, must never try to 'help'.

In the middle of the night, not knowing where she

82

was, she awoke in a panic, unable to get her breath. All she could see was a sharp crescent moon hanging over the western sky, about to dip behind the skeletal trees. She slipped out of bed, padding over to the window. She opened it to lean out into the night, taking long, deep breaths until the frosty air hit her lungs sharply, grounding her.

She gave herself a stern lecture as she returned to her bed. It was not a question of giving up a big house and all that went with it, including her memories of Peter, and the respect that went with the address. What about gaining the new lease of life, a new perspective on everything? The prospect, if she could allow herself to dwell on it, might be quietly thrilling.

Yet the week-end passed in a turmoil of doubt, of lectures to herself and of rehearsals in her mind of pulling out of the sale and the purchase. Her briefly sinking heart greeted Monday morning. Today was the day of change. A bright sky with crisp air mocked her. Until the appointed time that the small removal van was expected to be at the house, she remained at the hotel. A taxi took her to supervise the operations there.

Afterwards, came the most heart-wrenching part of the whole exercise, leaving the keys with the estate agency. The removal van arrived at Tarascon Court to pull up in the car park until instructed to begin moving furniture in. Feeling shaky, Lydia returned to the lounge at the hotel to await a phone call to tell her that all monies had reached their correct destinations. By now, it was after midday. She was hungry but couldn't eat. Another visit to the estate agency to collect the keys to number twenty-nine Tarascon Court and the worst was over. Or was it ahead?

The removal men had gone. Her much reduced

worldly goods were safely around her. Through the south-facing window of the living room, the sun beamed a welcome. She made herself a cup of tea and sat down to survey her home, her new, small, but compact home, telling herself, yes, it was good. She had done the right thing.

Or had she?

* * *

On Tuesday morning, the day after moving, Polly, on half term holiday from school, paid Lydia a visit. She came into the sun-lit living room, her eyes eager to recognise familiar items from the house. Polly was such a comfort.

"Oh, the sofa," she said falling onto it and smoothing its surfaces with her hands. "It's an old friend, isn't it? You haven't got any curtains."

"Would you like to come out with me to get some?"

"I'd love to. Why didn't you bring some from the house?"

"Too big. Too heavy. Anyway I'd like some new ones. How about tomorrow morning?" Polly nodded her approval.

Lydia hesitated in the doorway to the kitchen. "Lemonade?"

"Yes, please. Gran, are you okay?"

"I'm actually very okay. Pleased with myself."

"So you're not - not ill, or anything?"

"No. Why?"

Polly's eyes were searching for something. Lydia watched her.

"Why do you ask?" Lydia prompted.

"Those books. You know. The one's about, you know, about death."

"Books? Oh, the books, I know. Books about death and dying? Oh, Polly, I didn't realise. Did you think I was ill?"

The black rimmed eyes filled with tears. "Yes, I did. I thought you were going to die."

Lydia abandoned the lemonade to hurry over to her, to sit next to her on the sofa and put her arms around her. "Polly, dear, why didn't you say? I'm only reading about death because I should be prepared. It's not healthy to keep avoiding such truth. And it's not as frightening as you think."

"So you're not ill and you're not going to die?"

"Not yet. I will, one day. You must be prepared for that."

"You, die? Oh, never!" Polly's arms tightened around her with a ferocity that was both sad and amusing. Lydia knew, despite her amusement, she could not let Polly go, either. Polly filled her life, now, since the breakdown in the relationships with Kate and Ellie.

"I know that this is an old folks' place," Polly went on, "they all die here."

"Look," Lydia said, "I took two of those books with me to the hotel. I had a lovely week-end there, reading them and curing myself of my fear of death. I am enjoying reading them."

"Enjoying them?" Polly's eyes resisted the weight of their make-up and opened wide. "In a hotel? You have a weird way of enjoying yourself." She paused. "Thanks for the shepherdess," she added, curling up in the crook of Lydia's arm. "Are you sure you don't want her back? She'd look lovely in here."

"No, dear. She's yours."

"Then I'll redecorate my bedroom in white and grey and pale, pale blue to match her."

Lydia rose to fetch the lemonade. "What will Mum say to that?" she called from the kitchen.

"She'll say I keep changing my mind. Well, I do. I wanted to be a maths teacher a couple of weeks ago."

"And this week?" Lydia placed the glass of lemonade on the small table within Polly's reach.

"I want to go back to the idea of being a courier, you know, taking people abroad on holiday. Mr Hornby's left our school. I don't think I'll get my GCSE in maths now. I'm good at French so I'll concentrate on that. I'll never get over there 'cos of Dad's redundancy. I wanted to go on the school trip in the summer. To France."

"No money?"

Polly nodded.

"I'll pay. I'll pay for the school trip you wanted."

"Will you? Have you paid your mortgage?"

The lie! Lydia had forgotten her tactic to dissuade interest by the family in her finances. She wanted her daughters to have the money but was now reluctant to offer such help until the feud was over. Money muddied relationships.

"Yes. There's plenty left over to pay for your trip."

"Thanks, Gran. That's great. I was going to sell some of the jewellery."

So Polly had opened the second box as well. Lydia smiled. "You don't have to sell any of the jewellery."

"That's good, because I wanted to keep that. For my children. Its gold, isn't it?"

"Some of it is gold. Some of it is silver."

"Heirlooms, you know. I'll be able to say to my

children and my grandchildren, 'This belonged to my grandmother', won't I?"

"Suppose they're all boys?"

"They'll have wives, won't they, when they grow up?"

"You are planning ahead."

"I've already made a start."

"Made a start?" Lydia regarded her with alarm. "What on earth do you mean, Polly?"

Polly clasped her hands together and wriggled. "I've got a boy-friend," she announced, her face growing pink.

That would explain the dramatic make up. "Have you? What's his name?"

"Jez. Really he's Gerard Gorman. I told you about him. He's nice. He's in my class." She wriggled again. "He's my boy-friend now. I haven't told Mum yet. I haven't told her about the jewellery, either. She was in a foul mood all weekend. She opened that box of plates you gave her. She threw some of them at Dad. She'd been drinking. I ignored her."

Showing any reaction to this information would be a mistake. Lydia kept her voice light. "You shouldn't keep important things from her. You must tell her about the jewellery. And about the boy-friend. She thinks I'm trying to turn you against her."

"She can do that all by herself," Polly muttered. "You can tell her that."

"Does she know you're here?" Polly made no answer. "Please, Polly, tell her."

"Why don't you phone her now and tell her all that and say I'm not telling her things."

"I will. After you've left."

Polly was getting impatient with the conversation.

"Can I see the rest of the flat now, with your things in it?"

A while later she left with an arrangement to visit on Wednesday morning to go out with Lydia on a curtain-buying outing.

With no garden, not a lot of housework and despite unpacking waiting to be tackled, Lydia was able to stretch out on the sofa once Polly had gone. Through the window, she was able to see the sun shining through the treetops. A few of the trees around Tarascon Court were close enough for tight buds to be visible. February was nearly ended and March brought hope. Not that Lydia needed that. She marvelled at her contentment after all the anguish, all the doubt. Not preoccupied with the 'should I? Should I not?' inner dialogue about the move, she found herself debating whether or not to phone Kate. Moving was a good reason for making contact. And Kate had her half-term break.

So Lydia phoned her.

"Hello, Mum. You don't often use your mobile." That was good. She should have done this sooner.

"Hello, dear. How are you? It's all I have now, the mobile. I'm in my flat."

"Are you? Is it all to your pleasing? Thank you for the stuff you left. Dan was really pleased to have the collection of Wisdens. I don't know where he'll put them. He hasn't played cricket for donkeys' years. That doesn't count, though. Men are odd, aren't they?" Kate sounded cheerful, with no hint of the foul mood Polly had mentioned.

"Some are," Lydia agreed. "They were Peter's, you know, the Wisdens. And the dinner set? I know it's a bit old-fashioned so I don't mind if you sell it."

"Sell it?" She heard Kate take a deep breath and

remembered what Polly had told her about some of the dinner plates being thrown at Dan after she had been drinking...

"Yes. It's Royal Worcester."

"Ellie will come to pick up her box when she has time," Kate said. She clearly didn't want to talk about the Royal Worcester.

"Do you think she'd speak to me? I haven't heard from her or spoken to her for ages."

"I don't know. I haven't seen much of her lately. Nor of you. I've been taken up with..." Her voice trailed off. "School stuff and worry about Dan being made redundant. I don't seem to have the time." Kate maintained a long silence after that. "Polly's always out. She's got new friends. I don't know them. They're not from school."

"Polly was here earlier, Kate, but she's gone now. She told me about her boy-friend. I don't see much of her, you know. I'm not trying to turn her against you."

"I never for one moment thought you were."

"Kate, you suggested that when you spoke to me on Friday evening. That's really why I'm phoning."

"Did I?" Wariness crept into the voice.

"You phoned me. I was at the hotel. I think you had some strange idea that I had Polly with me."

"I don't remember. Is this true?"

"Yes, Kate. I can quite believe you don't remember. You sounded to me as though you were very much the worse for drink."

"What did I say?"

"Let me see," Lydia spoke slowly, then paused, not sure whether to continue.

"Are you still there?" Kate urged.

"Yes."

"I thought you'd put the phone down on me."

"Why would I do that? You asked me what you said, in your phone call. Let me tell you. I recall quite vividly, that you brought Peter into it."

"Did I?" That was a lame response.

"You referred to him as a gargoyle. Do you remember?"

"I'm sorry, Mum. I've been a bit busy lately, with one thing and another."

"Why don't you come and see my new flat?"

Silence.

"Why don't you?"

"I could, couldn't I?"

"It does take time, doesn't it?"

"What does?"

"Recovering from that much drink."

"Bye, Mum. Thanks for phoning." Kate ended the call. Lydia smiled to herself.

* * *

Polly kept her appointment with Lydia on Wednesday morning to go on the expedition to choose curtains for the flat. They headed for the 'ready-made' section of the haberdashery department of the town's large store. It was there that Polly spied Jane. All pleasure in the morning was sucked away in an instant.

"I don't want that girl to see me," she said, lurking behind hanging samples of curtain material.

"What girl?" Lydia looked around.

"Don't look!" Polly said, abandoning her choice of turquoise and gold stripes so that 'unguided', Lydia ended up with three pairs of curtains that were plain cream cotton.

"Which girl do you mean?" Lydia said.

"That one over there. In the silly high heels." Polly looked down, muttering to the floor. "It's Jane."

They moved away from the counter, the curtains, unapproved by Polly. Lydia asked what was the matter with seeing Jane.

"I'm disappointed in you, choosing those curtains. I'm upset at seeing Jane."

"Come and have a coffee with me in the coffee shop. And a scone if you want one."

Jane appeared again, in the coffee shop. An initially hostile glance from her changed into an uncertain smile. Polly's response was also an uncertain smile.

"Why didn't you want her to see you?" Lydia asked.

"Jane? She was my best friend until she went over to Cordelia's camp."

"And is she still in Cordelia's camp?"

"I don't know. I don't bother with her. I'm with Jez and his mates now. So it doesn't matter. Did you have bullying when you were at school?"

Lydia frowned. "I'm not sure, really. We had different attitudes to things then."

"What do you mean? No one was allowed to bully anyone else?"

"In a way. We were more in fear of authority than your generation. I can only think that that perhaps was the reason we didn't bully each other so much. We would have been bullied by teachers and such people, you know, corporal punishment."

"What's that? Caning?"

"And slapping, hitting. I got the ruler several times."

Polly sat forward, aghast. "A ruler? What for? Were you naughty?"

"Yes. Talking in class. Blotting my book. We had real ink, you see."

"That's cruel. Do you think it damaged you?"

"I don't think so, but I could be wrong."

"Mum said she and Ellie were damaged because you left their father for Peter. She said that happened because your mother left your father."

Lydia laughed. "I see. Your Mum would have been perfect but for that, would she? And I would be perfect if my mother hadn't left a wreck of a man who came back from the war almost unrecognisable."

"Why did you leave?"

"I protected both my girls from their father. I think I told you, didn't I, that he drank and was violent?"

"Sorry, I mentioned that to her, to Mum."

"What did she say?"

"She said it wasn't true. You left for Peter. Is he still alive?"

"You're grandfather? Drink killed him. Cirrhosis of the liver. Your Mum was twenty-two at the time. She knew. Tell me more about Jane. Why didn't you want her to see you?"

"Because…" Polly began. "Because she and Cordelia and Alice and Wanda, they're the ones who ganged up on me and called me fat. And I'm not fat. They tried to give me a tattoo and caused a lot of trouble for me. I was left all alone at school. I was very lonely, Gran." The tears began to spill as they left the coffee shop.

Out in the daylight now, mingling with the town shoppers. Lydia caught hold of Polly's arm and tucked it into hers.

Polly glanced up at her. "I'm upset about Jane. It was horrible being so lonely."

"I know about loneliness, Polly. After Peter died, I was so desperately lonely. I think Kate and Ellie didn't understand."

"You're not lonely now, though, are you, not now you live at Tarascon Court? I had no one to talk to at break. Until Jez."

"The boy-friend? And he's kind?"

"He is. I'm friends with his mates, as well. All my friends are boys, now. I'm like a gangsters' moll. Don't tell Mum."

"I won't. Does she not know?"

"About the boys? Being a gangsters' moll? No. But she wants me to invite Jez to tea. He's kind. He told me to keep a diary on my phone, of the bullying. He showed me how to do it." Polly began to laugh, a laugh that was a strange, almost teary laugh. "Jez, sitting down, drinking tea and eating cakes? That's hilarious."

"What would you rather do?"

"Burgers and coke."

"One day, you must bring him round to meet me."

Polly stopped, dragging Lydia back. People bumped into them. "Really? Oh, Gran. Thanks. That's lovely." She threw her arms round her grandmother.

"Mind! I'm in danger of losing my curtains. What do you plan for now? Would you like a burger and coke today?"

Polly hesitated to answer. They walked on in the direction of home.

"That's a lovely idea, Gran, but I promised Mum I'd be home in time for something to eat before I meet Jez this afternoon."

As Lydia entered the main door of Tarascon Court, the lift doors opened. Veronica's son, Ashton Hornby, emerged.

"How is Veronica?" she asked him.

He gave a faint shrug. "She's had three difficult days, keeping appointments at the hospital. We've not long come back from there. I'm doing a few chores." He held up a rubbish bin. "Curtains?" he asked, indicating the large carrier bag Lydia was holding.

"Yes. Just bought."

"Tell you what. When Mum is asleep, and I hope she will be soon, because she's exhausted, would you like me to pop up and help you hang them?"

"That would be very kind. I've got all the hooks and things that are needed."

He smiled. "And a little light stool or ladder?"

Lydia nodded and thanked him. She was preparing to make a cup of tea when she saw the bottle of wine, opened only the previous evening, to celebrate the move. She poured herself a glass, stretched herself out on the sofa to wait for her knight in shining armour to come to her aid with the curtains. She smiled to herself. How silly you became when safely old enough for it not matter.

A discreet tap on the front door announced Ashton's arrival. She let him in and showed him into the living room where a small ladder waited as well as all the hooks on the window sill.

She held up her glass. "I'll pour you one when you've done the curtains."

"That would be splendid," he said, removing his

jacket and draping it over the back of the sofa. She could smell him, his body odour and the scent of a preparation he used. She recalled Polly's observations about him.

"Actually," he said, "I'd really appreciate it now. I've had a terrible three days with Mum. She's fast asleep at the moment."

"Why? Is she distressed?"

"Oh, she's always distressed. She's not young, you know."

Lydia poured him a glass of wine. She noticed he had deft fingers. The hooks were fitted and fixed onto the rail in no time. He paused only to sip his wine, arranging the gathers at the top of the curtains then stepping down to admire his handiwork.

"Any more?" he said.

"Curtains or wine?" she laughed.

"Both."

"The other curtains are for the bedrooms," she said. The blue eyes met hers, the deft fingers touched hers as she handed him his refilled glass. She led him to her bedroom. He sat on the side of the bed. She sat next to him. He took a sip of wine before moving closer to her.

"Do you know, you are such an attractive woman?" he said and his arm coiled round her waist.

This might not be wise but it was wonderful. Was he sincere or was he mocking her? She turned to look at him, unable to curb the smile on her lips, unable to curb anything. He lifted her chin with gentle fingers and kissed her, only lightly, on the lips.

What was happening to her? This was the man who had been regarded by Polly her *grand-daughter*, as desirable. Feelings, sensations surged through her, over her, like a rip tide. He put his glass on the bedside table then tenderly he took her glass from her and placed it with his.

"Shall we?" he whispered and those hands, the deft fingers that had so competently and, yes, even erotically, fixed the curtains, were now caressing her neck, her shoulders. "I really do like older ladies. My former wife was fifteen years my senior."

The physical contact, the closeness of another human body, alive and pulsating, that was so exciting, confirming her own existence, her own life. But it was absurd, ridiculous, and worse, wrong. She was friends with his mother, for heavens' sake.

"No," she said, coming to her senses. "We shall not. I'm sorry if you think I've encouraged you, but I don't think this would be a good idea. Not only that, you apparently have a sick mother downstairs. It's not right. I'll go and make some coffee."

"Sure. I understand. No hard feelings, eh? Life's too short, I always think, but I respect your choice."

In half an hour, the coffee was made, drunk, the bedroom curtains hung and he was about to leave. At the door, he kissed her.

"Pretty delightful afternoon," he said. "In pretty delightful company. Maybe I can see you again sometime?"

She met those blue eyes without a flinch. "I think not, Ashton. Not even if your mother makes a miraculous recovery in the next five minutes. I'm sorry." Sorry? What was she saying? The man was a lecher. Thank God he was out of Polly's reach.

He left.

She stretched out on the sofa. That had been

ridiculous. Now she was uneasy. She felt she was young again and attractive. Not all of the encounter was regrettable. But how pathetic was she! A while later, she set out for choir practice. As she waited in the entrance hall for Clive to join her, Cathy appeared.

"How did it go?" she asked.

Lydia hesitated. What did the woman mean? Had she seen Ashton Hornby come to the flat? Or leave? Of course, she was referring to the move.

"Surprisingly well. So much less to worry about in this place. How was your trip?"

"Great. I always love a bit of time in London, so much energy, so much life. But I'm always glad to come home here, as well. How is Veronica? I know she had some hospital appointments."

"She's recovering, apparently. I haven't actually seen her since."

"You've met her son?" Cathy seemed amused.

"Yes, I have," Lydia said, trying not to flinch. And what a meeting…

* * *

"So how are you settling in?" Clive asked Lydia as they left Tarascon Court for the short walk to the church hall. It was Friday afternoon and Lydia had expressed her interest in the talks on ageing, The Wise Side of Life, taking place there.

"I've been busy, too busy to get to know people," Lydia said. "I've been sorting things out in my flat. It's small and my belongings fill it, so it's chaos. And that's after vigorous pruning. Tell me about the woman who gives these talks."

97

"Barbara Wills? She's not a great academic or anything like that. She's an ex- teacher. She said last week she became aware that she was ageing, she realised she had resisted Life all her life and started to go with this particular aspect of it. She did some reading and she wanted to share her discoveries."

"That could be any of us," Lydia said. The afternoon was bright. Spending it in a gloomy, old church hall could be a waste unless the message was important. Clive held the opinion that it was important.

"Have you ever," Barbara Wills began in her booming teacher's voice, "watched our contemporaries with their obsession with exercise? Have you seen the grey and bald heads bobbing along the river walk after nine o'clock in the morning?"

There was laughter.

"Then there's the over-sixties' yoga, the over fifty-fives' line-dancing here in this very hall. Of course, exercise is good for you, but in moderation, not in excess. But the obsession! The obsession of people of our age, with exercise, with trying to look younger than their actual age, with trying to maintain youth! And with all the other means of trying to be young or staving off old age. This obsession is not good. If you are lucky enough to reach old age, whenever you think it begins, and you haven't died young, it's here to stay, ageing, fool yourselves as you might. A well-lit mirror does not lie."

There was a ripple of uncertain laughter.

"Whether you like it or not, you are going to die."

A few titters braved the silence. Lydia indulged in a little private self-congratulation. She hoped to mend the rift between herself and her daughters before that occurred.

"Time to start living," boomed Barbara Wills.

That was what she had tried to do, Lydia told herself. She had started living since that wet evening when the bus had passed Tarascon Court with its warm and homely lit windows. Until that moment, she had been hanging onto Peter. Now she had let him go, hadn't she, even though she thought about him quite often.

"What we should be doing," Barbara Wills continued, "is exploring the depth of our lives, not the length."

This had an unexpected resonance for Lydia and was probably not at all what Barbara Wills had in mind. Her thoughts went back to Wednesday, to Ashton Hornby, a foolish impulse on his part, and nearly on her part, too, which she could have thought of as a betrayal of Peter by her. Yet, at the same time, it had been a kind of confirmation of herself, her being, her living in her body. She had no intention of allowing it again, and definitely not going further, and certainly not with Ashton Hornby. There was now an awkward barrier in her starchy friendship with Veronica, who was not at all well. Lydia needed to avoid Ashton, while the schools were closed, and which meant having to avoid Veronica also for the whole of half-term week.

"Doesn't mince her words," Clive was saying and Lydia became aware that she had missed significant points Barbara Wills had made. Never mind. If Barbara Wills could discover these truths, so too could Lydia Grover.

"Has anyone ever told you that looking at the past with regrets is morbid and worse, useless?" Barbara Wills was issuing another challenge. "All these young people telling their grannies how to suck eggs! Why do we listen? Look at the past, by all means, but look at it with new eyes, and a new heart."

Respect for the age of her audience and their physical difficulties, meant Mrs Wills' talks were short. While tea and biscuits were being served and the audience moved around and chatted, she moved around among them.

"Do you know," she addressed Lydia and Clive on one of these rounds, "when I was a teenager I was obsessed with opera and ballet. Once I embarked on a career, I forgot all that. No time. A disastrous marriage made those interests even more remote. But now I'm retired, I have rediscovered them. I take advantage of the live streamed performances of opera, ballet and drama at the local cinema. Wonderful. You always get a second chance."

"I suppose that's why I am in the choir," Clive said to Lydia. "I was in my school choir."

"I was, too, at my school," Lydia laughed. "She must be right. Time I discarded the books on dying and started really living. Not so much time ahead of us now to make up for lost opportunities."

Clive nodded in agreement. "I think she's saying we should rediscover the past, not make up for what it was like. Perhaps it was not like we think it was."

Later, after contemplating consulting the past, and Kate's and Ellie's possible interpretations of it, she gave attention again to the future. "Have you ever thought about dying?" she said to Clive.

He laughed. "You make it sound like an option. Or, on a par with the question, 'have you ever thought of dancing?' But, yes, actually, I have. I've even arranged my funeral, you know, including readings and music."

"The whole of Verdi's Requiem?"

"Not even an excerpt. There won't be many there, I can assure you, I am persona non grata in my family, what's left of them."

"What then?"

"'In Paradisum', from *Faure's Requiem*." His eyes were glancing around the hall as he spoke. "And stuff that will covey that I'm a decent bloke. That I'm not what they think, my relatives. A lot of them have gone themselves, now. But I mean the one or two that might turn up."

She watched him. The words were a protest, at the same time an attempt to be jocular. He was avoiding her gaze, then abruptly, turned to look at her, sheepishly.

"Tough life," he said. He paused, drew in a deep breath, and adding in a quiet voice, "My partner died, twelve years ago. He –," he stumbled on the small but significant pronoun, "He died without any of his family coming near him, out of six surviving siblings at that time, not one came to the funeral. I will have a similar end. It's the generation, you see, our generation. Nigel and I, we were gay long before the laws altered, before all the laws changed in our favour. He died before our partnership could have any of the benefits they do now. I was left homeless. The property, which was his, went to his eldest brother. It wouldn't happen now."

They were both silent for a while. Lydia stared into her teacup. She put a hand on his arm. "Clive, thank you for telling me this."

"You don't mind?"

"Mind? Quite the opposite."

"I didn't want you to be getting ideas."

"On the contrary, I'm sort of relieved." She couldn't

cope with another approach like Ashton Hornby's. Not yet. "You're safe, you know and do you remember I told you I had problems in my family? They are not resolved. I need to have a talk with you, if you would agree."

"I'd rather not invite you to my flat. They are hungry for gossip, some of our neighbours."

Thoughts were flashing across Lydia's brain like headlines. Ellie. Peter's son. This was a meaningful encounter, this meeting with Clive. Someone to talk to at last. And he was safe. After Wednesday, and Ashton Hornby, flattering though it had been, she was now aware of a new vulnerability, wondering at Ashton's motives. Rich widows, she thought, were a great attraction to preying Lotharios. Not that she was rich, not that rich. Maybe, though, her financial assets made her rich enough for some men.

"How about lunch out one day?" Clive was saying. "Next Friday. Before we come here?"

So long to wait. "That would be lovely," she said.

"I tend to avoid pubs. Do you know the restaurant on the top floor of the large store in town? How about there? Mid-day."

Her life was really beginning to sort itself out.

* * *

What did you do on a beautiful Sunday afternoon with no one with whom to share it? Lydia decided to go for a walk, down by the river. She was learning to be happy with her own company. While no longer did she grieve so painfully for Peter, for his company, the disagreement between herself and Ellie and Kate still hurt her.

She wandered along the river bank, her mind crammed with thoughts. The March sunshine had some warmth so she sat on the bench, lifted her face to it and closed her eyes. She would never have thought she could be so at peace on her own. She was learning.

"Hello," said a voice.

She perceived a slight movement of the bench as someone's weight was lowered on to it. She opened her eyes. A stranger sat next to her, smiling and studying her with concern, a dark stranger with shining eyes.

"Are you okay now?"

"Okay?" Then she remembered. "Oh, you're the bus driver, aren't you? You were so good when I wasn't well. I'm so grateful."

"Glad to be of help. I take it you have recovered?"

Lydia laughed. "I wasn't really ill. Stress, anxiety, they said at the hospital."

"Stress and anxiety? That's illness all right. But you've recovered?"

"Willpower. Talking to myself. Realising a few truths. Trying to be honest with myself. Reading a bit. Letting things go that are no longer useful or not my business."

"Wow! I wish I could do all that."

"I wish I could! But that's what I need to do. I haven't seen you on the bus recently."

The young woman sighed, turned her attention to the sun-sparkled river. "No, I've not been well. Stress and anxiety. It can do funny things to you."

"As I found out. I'm sorry to hear this. You struck me as being so upbeat. What was it you said about facing difficulties? If you feel down, don't fight it. Let it live until it dies, otherwise it'll come up and grab you when you're not looking. So I did that. More or less."

"I should take my own advice, shouldn't I? I think it's come up and grabbed me. My name is Rosemary, by the way."

"Good to meet you, Rosemary. I'm Lydia."

"Linda?"

"No, Lydia. It was an ancient kingdom in western Turkey."

"Unusual," Rosemary said with a smile that belied her claim to be suffering from stress and anxiety.

"You look and sound so cheerful," Lydia said.

"I'm afraid not to. I'm afraid take my own advice. Suppose I give in to it and never get back to normal?"

Lydia decided to take the risk. "I'm talking out of the top of my head here, so don't take me too seriously. But what if, what you think of as normal, is not good enough for you. What if you are meant to be better than mere normal?"

Rosemary looked shocked, then beamed a warm smile. "I'll need to consider that one," she said.

"So will I," Lydia said. Had she been trying too hard to be what she had considered a 'normal' person? To do it all 'right'? What would be better than that? To do what she needed?

They said goodbye and each went their own way, Lydia contemplating a role for herself that, at her age, or perhaps, appropriately at her age, involved being free of the compulsion to help, the compulsion to be involved, in particular, in her own family. In other words, minding her own business. That was a tough assignment.

* * *

104

Ashton had not been to see his mother since Wednesday afternoon. Observation of the car park from her window had suggested that to Lydia, for there had been no sign of the yellow sports car, though she could have missed him when she was out. By Sunday evening, she was sure Veronica would welcome a visitor.

"Oh, how nice to see you," Veronica said as she answered the door to Lydia's discreet tap. "I thought you were Ashton. I haven't seen him all week, not since the hospital. Do come in."

Lydia was already in. "I'm sorry I haven't been down. I had assumed Ashton had been here all half-term."

"Not a whisper from him. I don't know what I've done to upset him. He is somewhat unpredictable. Marguerite used to say that. Do sit down. Tea or sherry?"

"Sherry, I think, please, Veronica. I'm sorry I'm calling so late but I wanted to see how you are and I've been so busy. I had assumed Ashton was keeping an eye on you." Now there was the concern that it was somehow her fault that Ashton had stayed away. "Who is Marguerite?"

"His wife. Ex-wife, now. She was so wrong for him, but she was perceptive. She saw things about Ashton that I missed. He is unpredictable, as I said. I could see no fault in him, you see."

Lydia accepted a glass of sherry and sank down onto the other recliner chair. "You don't, with your own children, do you?" Not unless, she reflected, their actions force you to do so. "Tell me about Marguerite."

"She was so wrong for my Ashton. He was only young. She was fifteen years older than him. I saw her as a rival mother. I think she saw herself that way, too. But she was quite well off, you know. Oh, yes, money was part of the attraction there, on my Ashton's part. Naughty boy." Veronica's faded blue eyes gazed into the distance.

"I suppose it was the age difference that caused the split?" Lydia said.

"Age difference, my foot," Veronica burst out with unexpected ferocity. "It was the affairs. He was always going off with some woman, Ashton was. Don't tell anyone, will you? Because I'd rather other people didn't know."

"Of course not. I understand."

"I often thought it was my fault. We mothers, we blame ourselves, don't we? But it was his fault. Totally his fault. He's charming and so good-looking, you see."

Lydia had seen and had been all but seduced by the charm and the good looks. So, it was true about the age of his ex-wife. The possibility that that story, about his ex-wife being sixty years old, had been a lie, had occurred to her. She leaned back to take a sip of sherry. Veronica was sitting in the light of a table lamp. Lydia watched her. She gave the appearance of being more frail than ever and when she turned to smile at her, Lydia was sure she was even thinner than when she had last seen her. Veronica was ill and Ashton did not care. And the sudden softening of her personality, the confidences, signified something.

Veronica fell asleep. Lydia covered her with a crochet shawl and left her. The time was half-past ten.

* * *

106

At eight o'clock the next morning she checked on Veronica.

"I'm fine," Veronica assured her. "I woke at about one o'clock, took myself off to bed and woke again at seven. Thank you so much for knocking."

Lydia hesitated. "Is there anything you need? I'm aware that you haven't been out and Ashton hasn't called. And it's Monday. He'll be at school again, won't he?"

"No, thank you. I need nothing but Ashton. He will call soon and anyway I'm well stocked up here. My freezer is full. Thank you so much."

The rest of the day for Lydia was spent disposing of cardboard boxes and the newspapers she had used for packing for the move. At half-past four there came a tap on the front door. Thinking it was Veronica in need of a drop of milk or something, she answered.

It was Ashton.

He smiled his warm, seductive smile. "Hello, Lydia. How are you?"

"I'm fine, thank you, which is more than can be said for your poor mother."

"I know." He tilted his head to one side. Over his shoulder, Lydia spied Cathy, the neighbour, about to enter the lift. "Poor Mum, as you say. But poor Ashton, too, you know. I'd very much like to repeat last Wednesday's little experiment –."

"No, thank you. Certainly not. I told you. Now I'm shutting this door. Go back to your mother."

"Aw!" He put his foot in the door as Lydia was about the close it.

"Move your foot," she spat at him. "This is harassment. I've just seen my neighbour go by. Now get out before I scream."

"I do love an assertive woman," he said, smiling calmly. He removed his foot. She slammed the door. About ten minutes later, the door bell rang. Lydia rushed across the room to the hall. She didn't wait to check through the spy hole, but snatched the door open. It was not Ashton. It was Cathy.

"Lydia, can I have a chat with you?"

Lydia hesitated. She was reluctant to appear too friendly, because she suspected the woman wanted to see what was in her flat, a suspicion that had resulted from living alone in a big house for five years and had been reinforced by Veronica's wariness about the neighbours. She did a quick rethink.

"Yes, of course. Do come in. I'm sorry if I have appeared to be stand-offish, but I've been so busy."

"Oh, I know. I've not been here long myself. I remember. You find you have so much stuff that's unnecessary, don't you?"

Cathy made herself comfortable on the sofa, indicating that she might be there for some time. Lydia offered her tea.

"Oh, I don't think so, thanks, Lydia. I love it up here on the top floor, don't you?"

"It's a wonderful view," Lydia agreed, perched on the edge of her chair.

"You know, when I was young," Cathy went on, "I kept taking photos on holidays, of my kids. I thought I would be spending my old age going through them, being nostalgic, you know? And guess what? I can't be bothered to look at them and recall those feelings I had then. I was so troubled, frustrated, hard up, anxious. But life's lovely now, serene, tranquil. Do you know Ashton Hornby?"

The question came without warning, tacked on the end of volubility about nostalgia.

"Only because I've known Veronica for some time."

"I don't want to gossip...."

Lydia was sure she didn't want to gossip but was going to do so anyway.

"... but he has a reputation, you know."

"What kind of reputation? Well-known?"

"Not really. Well hidden, I'd say. Only to those who know." Cathy paused. "For sexual conquests. Of older women, mostly."

Lydia felt herself growing hot. "That's unusual, isn't it? I mean, men, older and younger, are usually looking for younger women. Older women stand little chance with older men."

"True. Which makes him a bit suspicious. He married one, you know, an older woman. She was quite well off. But she divorced him and took him to the cleaners."

"Is this true?"

"It is. He lived in different places around the country, and moved his mother to retirement flats where he thinks, or hopes, there are lots of rich widow's. Well, he's done it three times, anyway. I know because he tried it on with my sister, Teresa. She lives in a retirement flat in London."

Cathy paused and glanced down at her fidgety hands in her lap. She lifted her eyes to meet Lydia's. "He tried it on with me," she said, her distressed face fiery red, "he tried it on and I'm ashamed to say he succeeded. More than once. I was so stupid, and flattered, of course. When I first moved here, he helped me, hanging curtains, moving furniture, shifting boxes. I was so stupid. I told Teresa. She was horrified. 'He's a lecher', she said to me."

Lydia sat as if frozen. Was this gossip? Was it motivated by envy, sexual jealousy? That was a strange thing to think. Perhaps Cathy was trying to spoil something. Well, there was nothing to spoil.

Afraid of her message being dismissed, Cathy said, "I saw him at your door earlier."

Lydia hadn't moved. When she did, she covered her face with her hands. "Oh, no, Cathy, I'm the latest."

"I wasn't quick enough, then. I'm sorry. Don't feel bad. He's to blame, not you."

"I feel stupid. But I came to my senses just in time, you know? It felt wrong, with his mother sick and her being so friendly with me."

"He's a fast worker, isn't he? Irresistible, I know. You've only been here a week. I'm not making trouble, Lydia. Honestly. The man is dangerous in places like this. Older people are always thought of as easy targets, aren't they, for all sorts of scams and deceits."

Lydia removed her hands from her face. "I feel so – so – stupid. Thank God I stopped him."

"Well, don't feel stupid. I refuse to be a victim. We'll get the bastard, won't we, somehow?"

Lydia nodded. Kind though she was, she wished Cathy would stop talking. Thoughts, difficult to acknowledge thoughts, were plaguing her from somewhere deep down inside her, a dark place but there were truths there.

"Cathy, thank you so much for telling me all this. And for being so honest. But I have some thinking to do. I need to be honest with myself about this and about other stuff, too."

Cathy rose. "I hope I haven't upset you."

"No, no. It's not that. Do you go to the talks in the church hall, *'The Wise Side of Life'*? On Fridays, they are. The speaker made a comment that I haven't given much thought to until now. She said that Socrates said, 'the *unexamined life is not worth living*'. I didn't really understand. But now I think I need to examine my life."

"Can I pop in tomorrow to check you're okay? For my own sake, to be honest."

"Of course, of course. I'd be pleased to see you."

Cathy left. Lydia stretched out on the sofa, closing her eyes. In her mind she returned to the lunch party at Kate's some weeks earlier. Ellie had been so happy until Lydia had expressed her doubts about the news. Yes, she had valid reasons for being concerned about Ellie's new life path. The jibe from Ellie, about her not valuing sex had rankled. *'Two children and two marriages and you don't understand the power and the loveliness of sex'*. At the time, Lydia had thought how wrong Ellie was, but it was difficult to say that. The memory had returned on several occasions.

And now, she had compounded this problem with Ellie by giving her that box. It contained, well – absolute dynamite with regard to Ellie's life, and to her relationship with her mother.

She hoped there was a chance that Ellie had not opened it. She had to get that box or its contents back. Much would depend on what Clive said on Friday when they had lunch. There was nothing for it but to acknowledge, if she wanted a better, more mature understanding between herself and her daughters, that part of her motive for disturbing Ellie had been a twinge of sexual jealousy.

* * *

Tuesday dawned a bright spring day. From her personal nest at the top of Tarascon Court, Lydia had a literal birds' eye view of their activities. Watching the birds, their busyness, their certainty, was balm for the soul. In a box, still packed, she had a book about identifying birds. Yet, why bother with organising her thoughts about them, she was there, with them, enjoying them. Labels could have taken the joy out of that.

After a slight breakfast, she hurried down one floor to check on Veronica. Ashton would not be there. The school term had resumed. On school days, he called in after five o'clock at the earliest.

Lydia tapped on Veronica's door. Twice. When there was no reply, she pressed the bell, lightly at first, more firmly the second time. Harsh ringing inside the flat could be heard in the corridor, loud enough to wake the dead. What? Oh, no, not that! Yet there have been a different attitude in Veronica on Sunday evening, a reckless confiding, and openness not typical of her at all.

Lydia gave up. The time was past eight o'clock. The manager would have arrived by now so she went down in the lift to the office.

Sue said little but looked serious. She took a master key from a locked cupboard and accompanied Lydia back up to the fourth floor. She unlocked Veronica's front door. Lydia followed her into the flat.

Veronica was there, easily seen from the hall, through the open door of the living room, sitting in her recliner chair, fully dressed in her favourite pastel colours, her head tilted into the wing of the chair. She looked utterly peaceful.

112

"Oh, I say," Sue said.

"Oh dear," Lydia murmured, adding, "Doesn't she look lovely?"

Sue touched one of Veronica's hands that resting on the arm of the chair. "Ice cold," she said. "She must have gone during the night."

Ashton had visited only briefly yesterday, Monday evening, Lydia knew. She had kept a watch for his car, in order to avoid him. It had stayed in the car park for less than ten minutes, and most of those ten minutes had been taken up with him trying to engage her interest. She touched the ice-cold hand. Veronica appeared empty, empty of life. No more waiting for Ashton, no more fooling herself about him. And for Ashton, no more unconditional love. Lydia now had another reason to be angry with him, his neglect, his disinterest in his doting mother. Poor Veronica.

"I'll go down to the office and phone her doctor," Sue said. "Then I expect she'll be taken away. Thank you, Lydia, for your concern about her."

Sue held the front door open for her. Lydia hung back. She had to have a last glimpse of Veronica, sitting in her favourite chair, every hair perfectly in place, even in death.

She returned upstairs to her own flat where she made herself some coffee and sat on the sofa contemplating death. Veronica had looked so peaceful, as Peter had, when he died. She recalled what she had read in her library books, about death. It was not spectacular, but was quiet, a quiet event, nothing alarming, nothing dramatic. She wished she had been less afraid at Peter's death. She had been there, holding his hand while he just slipped away. His pain, far from increasing as she had imagined it would, left him. How she missed him, his calmness, his warmth, his sheer enjoyment of life. Poor Veronica. She never gave the impression of enjoying life, rather she was too consumed with anxiety about doing the right thing, about what people thought of her.

From the living room window, she saw the doctor arrive, then Ashton's car appeared. She drew back, even though she was five floors up and entirely out of reach or vision. It was shame rather than fear, remorse rather than anger that moved her. The private ambulance arrived, with its discreetly blacked out windows. Veronica was loaded, like any luggage, in any vehicle, and off she went.

A while later, Cathy tapped on the front door. Lydia was wary and peeped through the spy hole, not wanting to be caught by Ashton, unprepared, again. Cathy had said yesterday she would call. She had a sensitive conscience and was a totally honest woman, Lydia decided.

"I know I said I'd pop in to see if you're okay," she said, "but I also want to know who was taken away in the private ambulance. Was it Veronica?"

Lydia confirmed that it was and invited her in but Cathy was busy, with her sisters, nieces and nephews, not to mention her own brood, now adult. Cathy was not lonely. After being reassured that Lydia had not been disturbed by her information about Ashton and by Veronica's death, Cathy left, pronouncing the taking away of Veronica's body as 'gruesome'.

Later that morning, Lydia had a phone call that surprised her. She lifted the phone, "Hello?"

There was a long silence at the other end. She

repeated her greeting, about to glance at the screen to see if she recognised the caller's number.

"Mum…" An uncertain voice mumbled.

"Kate? It's lovely to hear from you. How are you?" Lydia was aware of her own robust voice in contrast to Kate's hoarseness.

"Mum?" Kate said again.

"Yes, dear?" Lydia waited. Kate sounded as if she was crying. There were sniffs and throat clearing.

"Mum, I'm in trouble…"

"Are you? Do you want to tell me?"

"Not really. I'm so ashamed."

"Nothing is that bad, Kate."

"No. No, I suppose you're right."

"Would you like to come round to me?"

"And see the flat? Yes, I would. Shall I come straight away, if it's okay with you."

"Of course. In about ten or fifteen minutes? I'll come down and wait for you by the main door."

Lydia left the phone on her table, looked around the flat to check that everything was in order, then remembered a request she could make to Kate. She rang her.

"You haven't left yet, thank goodness."

"About to. What is it, Mum?"

"That box. The one for Ellie. The small one. Has she opened it yet?"

"No, it's still here."

Lydia heaved a sigh of relief and sent up thanks to whatever deity had arranged that. "Would you mind bringing it with you? There's something in it I need now. I put it in by mistake, that's all."

"I'll bring it. I know exactly where it is."

Lydia thanked her and went to keep watch from her window. Beyond the entrance to the flats, the road was visible.

When spring finally arrived and the leaves opened, the view would be a mass of green. Even the river would be hidden by the chestnuts, elms and beech trees. The prospect was exciting, watching spring spilling and emerging from this height. Already the crows were nesting high in the elms, like black litter among the delicate lace of the twigs and branches.

Kate was easily spotted, a stooped figure, hands in pockets, the box under her arm, hair wild, walking erratically. Lydia's heart went out to her. Kate was suffering, she was a picture of pain.

Lydia hurried down in the lift. When she opened the door and saw her, she was shocked. A white face, dark shadows, dead eyes, confronted her. She wanted to embrace her, hug her hard, let some of her own life and energy flow into her daughter. All she said to her, all she dared to say was, "Hallo, dear."

Kate gazed at her. Lydia expected her to cry.

"Hallo, Mum," Kate said. "I've got the box."

"Thank you." Lydia made no attempt to take the prettily wrapped box from Kate. She led her to the lift and up to the flat.

"Seems nice here," Kate said looking round as they emerged from the lift onto the landing.

"It's fine," Lydia said.

Once in the flat, Kate held out the box. "What's in it?"

"A bit of jewellery, a few mementoes, photos, that's all. There are a couple of items I wished I hadn't parted with. Thank you for bringing it. Why don't you sit down, dear, and I'll make some coffee."

"Do you have a drink? I'm in a bit of a state."

"I have some sherry. I bought it for Veronica but she died last night."

"That's a shame," Kate said. Whether she meant it was a shame about the sherry not going to its destination, or Veronica going to hers, was not clear. Kate sank onto the sofa, Lydia perched on her chair.

"Kate, are you drinking a lot lately?" She had to broach the subject.

"Not really. Why?"

"Your last phone call, before today, I mean, you sounded as though you'd had rather a lot to drink."

"Oh, that."

"Because your father drank, you know."

"Dad? He drank?"

"To excess."

"When?"

"All the time."

"Really? We didn't know, me and Ellie. We didn't suspect a thing."

"I made sure you didn't." Too much scrutiny of Kate's life might not be well received.

"Have you met Polly's boyfriend, yet?"

"Yes, and he's very nice. Polite, helpful. I'm sort of relieved. I thought she might go for some drug-pushing creep who would abuse her. Though I know there's plenty of time for that."

"Shouldn't you be at school today? Half-term's over, surely."

Kate burst into tears.

Lydia moved to the sofa, to sit next to her and to put a tentative arm round her shoulders. Rigid, Kate sat there, dabbing her tears.

"I went to the doctor this morning. She's signed me off work. I'm not to go back until she says."

"That's good." Lydia was careful with her responses. The repair to the relationship had made a start, precarious though it was. Spoiling it would be so easy. "You'll be able to have a rest for a while. You work hard."

Kate took several sips of her sherry. Kate scanned the living room, her eyes searching for the familiar. "Can I see round the flat, now, Mum?"

Lydia moved back to her chair. It was time to change the subject yet again. Kate was avoiding going further than the surface of anything. She had something to hide.

"Of course. This is the living room, as you can see. Through there is the kitchen, small but beautifully formed."

Kate put her head round the kitchen door. "What else?" she said. She was led out to the small hall, to admire the ample storage space and cupboards, and followed Lydia into the bedrooms. In the larger bedroom, Ashton Hornby came vividly to Lydia's mind. He was her shameful secret. Kate inspected the bathroom.

"It's very small," Kate said. "Are you feeling a bit squashed after the big house?"

"Not really. It feels good to have offloaded so much that is not necessary. There's not a lot to worry about. Look, Kate, I want to apologise for the way I reeled off about yours and Ellie's behaviour twenty-five years ago."

Kate stared at her. "No, Mum. We deserved what you said. It was true. Both of us, we were a right pair of bitches. Please don't take it back. It was awful, what we put you through. We never really understood why you didn't come down on us like a ton of bricks then."

Lydia blinked. All that angst for nothing?

They returned to the living room where Kate, like everyone else, was drawn to the view from the window.

"Lovely view," she said, attempting a smile. "It's worth a lot, a view like this, isn't it?" She glanced back to the car park. "Nice big car park."

"Kate," Lydia began. "I really feel I ought to explain---."

"Oh, my God!" Kate was staring down to the car park. "Oh, my God! What's he doing here? He should be in school."

Lydia rose quickly, stumbling in her haste. "Who? What?"

Kate's shaking finger pointed to a distinctive yellow car. "Him. That car. It's Ashton Hornby's."

"Do you know him?"

"Do I know him!" Kate burst out. She turned away from the window. "He's the cruellest bastard who ever lived on this earth. I hate him. I really, absolutely, hate him."

For a moment, Lydia was numbed, wondering what Kate could possibly mean because surely nobody could have told her about the encounter with Ashton Hornby last Wednesday. Gathering her dithering wits, she pursued Kate, stumbling in her haste to reach her and to lead her back to the sofa. Kate threw herself down onto it. Her face was contorted with rage, her fists pummelled everything around her.

"What's he doing here? He should be in school. I thought I was safe today, to come here, to see you, to get everything sorted."

Lydia sat down beside her and tried to put her arms round Kate's writhing, angry body. But she would not be still.

"I told you," Lydia said, speaking in a low voice and trying to use a calm tone, "I told you. His mother lived here. She died. He would have taken time off, to sort things out. Is he a teacher at your school?"

"I worked with him," Kate said, beside herself with fury. "In the same classroom. I was his teaching assistant. We worked well together. We – we grew very close. I can't keep the job now."

Kate relaxed unexpectedly and leaned into her mother's shoulder. Lydia stroked her hair and mopped her tears. As Lydia continued to hold her, she quietened.

"I'll tell you," Kate murmured into her mother's shoulder. "I'll tell you. I knew his mother lived here. I didn't know she had died. Me and Ashton, well, we became close. We got on so well. He gave me a lift home every day after school. Then, on the Friday before half-term, he took me for a drink, several drinks as it happened, at the White Hart, just past Ellie's. It was to thank me for my support. I got very drunk. I didn't realise. That was when I phoned you, I think. I don't remember clearly."

Lydia hardly heard a word Kate was saying after Ashton's name. The repugnance the name induced in her caused nausea. He had used her poor Kate not only in the way he had tried to use her, but far more callously, by the sound of it.

She made no comment, but sat with her arms around her daughter. There was nothing she could say.

"It went on from there," Kate continued, "every day

in half-term I went to his flat. Dan was on late shifts, Nick is leading his own life, and Polly has got herself a nice boy-friend. I was able to go up to Ashton's flat. I've got to say it, Mum, and I resent the fact at the same time, but it was bloody marvellous. I didn't know it could be like that."

As she realised what Kate was saying, Lydia's arms tightened round her. She now was, herself, quietly railing against Ashton Hornby. Not that she had doubted her but Cathy had been quite right. He was a lecher, a Don Juan, a cynical user of women.

A great sigh escaped from Kate. "I didn't know, Mum. Dan's not up to that. He knows nothing. I'm so angry with him, too. Like Ellie said, marriage and two children and *I* didn't appreciate, you know…"

Kate's raw face lifted to meet Lydia's eyes. "Are you disgusted with me? Are you shocked?"

"No, dear. Of course not. We all make mistakes. I'm sorry you are so upset, though."

"I got tired Sunday. When we went back to school yesterday, it was awful. I could hardly keep my eyes open I was so tired. On Sunday night and Monday night I left Dan in bed and went to Ashton's. He picked me up his car, on the main road. Honestly, Mum, I felt like a prostitute when I got into that car. I said so to him and he laughed and said my skirt was not short enough and my heels not high enough and I thought, and I think I said to him, how did he know? That thought has kept coming back to me. Last night, I was so absolutely exhausted, and he changed."

Kate sat bolt upright and turned to regard Lydia. "Are you disgusted with me? Are you sure you're not disgusted with me?"

"No, dear. I told you. Have another sip of your sherry and I'll tell you a story."

Not to be distracted, Kate continued to gaze at Lydia in disbelief. "It's been a terrible year, what with redundancy, the worry about money. The only good thing was going on at school. He was utterly, utterly charming, all the time. The kids loved him. I thought I did until last night."

"He's only charming when he gets his own way, is that it?"

"I think so. Tell me your story."

"Don't berate yourself, Kate. I've done exactly the same thing, you know. Even to the slipping out at night and creeping back the next morning to get Ellie to school."

"With Peter?"

"With Peter. But it didn't end like your little adventure. It went on for months. Several nights a week I was doing that, for quite a while. It was wonderful. I felt alive, energised. Like Dan, your father was not wised-up to how women function. And he slept the sleep of a drunk. He drank a lot. He kept us poor and was often violent. I put up with a lot. I thought for a long while it was the right thing to do, you know, a woman had to sacrifice her own needs and honour her marriage vows."

"What rot. But then, that's what I've done. Dan, he spends money like water. I dread him getting his hands on any cash, it goes like it's slippery. We're thousands in debt, Mum. Surely you must realise?"

"The bathroom ceiling, it did make me think."

"It makes me sick," Kate said.

They were both silent for a few minutes.

"I want to tell you about Peter," Lydia said.

"You told Polly a bit about him. She told me."

"Unlike your little adventure, mine was with a caring man. In the end, I moved in with him. I took a protesting Ellie with me. You and she tried so hard to break it up, but even with that, I was so much happier, so much more relaxed."

"I remember when you went. I was working and living in London for a while. I came down to find you gone."

"I wasn't expecting you."

"I raised merry hell. I'm sorry, Mum. I understand a bit now. I wish I hadn't wasted myself on Ashton Hornby, though."

"All I can say is, I agree and understand what Ellie meant when she spoke of the power and loveliness of sex."

A smile crept over Kate's ruined face. "So she was wrong when she said that to you, that you didn't know."

Not blushing under Kate's gaze was difficult. She was well aware that she belonged to a generation with puritanical values, some of which still lurked deep in her. She didn't have the easy attitude to these matters that her daughter's generation did, and they, in turn, weren't as free as Polly's generation.

"Thanks, Mum for listening, for being understanding and telling me about – you know – Peter."

Lydia rose. "Go and give your face a splash of cold water in the bathroom. I'll make some sandwiches then we'll get you a taxi to take you home so you can avoid that lecher." Lydia glanced out of the window. "He's gone but that doesn't mean he won't be back. He's plundering Veronica's flat, I think."

"Can I stay longer? Dan doesn't know I'm not school. I'd rather take my time telling him – you know, stuff."

"Do you feel obliged to tell him?"

"I'll have to tell him. I'm leaving him."

"I see," Lydia said.

In the kitchen she prepared some cheese sandwiches and made a pot of coffee. Kate fell silent. When Lydia returned with a tray, she was asleep, stretched out on the sofa and there was an opportunity to sit in silence and deal with the conflict inside her. There was a lot to tell Kate. The topic of Ashton Hornby was not one she would have anticipated arising. Telling Kate about her little adventure with him last Wednesday might sooth Kate's ruffled soul. Or it might increase her rage and disgust with her mother and arouse a deeper sense of betrayal than Ashton had. But there were other things to tell her, an apology to be made.

Kate woke a while later.

"Sorry, I fell asleep. I didn't mean to."

Her glance lighted on the box that had been destined for Ellie.

"What's in there?" she said.

"I'll have to have a look to refresh my memory. Then I'll return it to her. I suppose I could go round to her. Would she slam the door in my face?"

"Probably not. But leave it a while. She has problems."

Lydia froze. "She's not ill, is she?"

"No, no. Rosie has moved in with her. She's not too well. Don't go round until she agrees. Phone her, if you must. But be careful how you deal with her, won't you?"

As soon as Kate left, Lydia took Ellie's box over to the table in the window. She ripped off the flowery gift wrapping and lifted the lid. Inside were the items she had packed for Ellie, Wedgwood Jasperware in more than adequate tissue, an envelope of photographs of Ellie as a child, small boxes of jewellery, earrings, rings, and a package in a purple envelope.

She selected the purple envelope, replaced the lid and pushed the box across the table away from her. She tipped the envelope's contents onto the table top – two photographs of a young man with hair in the style of three decades earlier, a press cutting and two further well-worn envelopes containing letters. She unfolded the tattered press cutting. A handwritten date, May nearly twenty-eight years ago was at the top above the headline. Below that was another photograph of the same young man. Underneath it was his name, Gary Grover. An account of the inquest into the death of Gary Grover, aged seventeen, followed. He had been found hanged. He left a note explaining his state of mind.

She refolded the cutting. That young man had suffered terribly at the hands of his peers and of his elders and betters. No one had understood him and his problem. He had been desperate for help and hadn't known where to turn and feared his mother's rejection and his father's disapproval. Peter's anguish over the death of his son lasted until his own death five years ago. Since they had met, the minds of herself and Peter had registered all suicides they heard about and even now, this continued for Lydia.

The press cutting and its accompanying letters were returned to the purple envelope. She was relieved Ellie had not read them. The inclusion of them had been thoughtless, if not cruel. Yet, how else, after that lunch party could she have responded, knowing about Gary and needing to express her concerns to Ellie? That both Ellie and Kate had leapt to the conclusion that she actually disapproved of Ellie's lifestyle had been a shock to her as had their aggressive attempts to stop her explaining. Any deeper motives on her part were disguised by her self-righteous sense of having been misjudged. Crossed wires, due to mistaken expectations, on both sides.

Lydia sighed her regret, wrapped the box in a different wrapping paper and put it back on the bookshelf until she could give it to Ellie personally. The purple envelope she slipped into her handbag. She glanced at her watch. Half-past eleven. On Friday she would be meeting Clive for lunch at the restaurant on the top floor of the town's department store. That meeting could not come quickly enough.

* * *

She arrived at the restaurant some minutes after mid-day. Clive was already at the table. He rose, as he saw her, to give her a peck on the cheek when she reached him.

"Now, tell me what you wanted to ask me?" he said when they both had a light lunch before them and had commented on the wet and windy weather.

She put down her knife and fork. "It's like this, Clive. My daughter, Ellie, recently announced that she was gay and I responded with less than enthusiasm."

Clive looked thoughtful. "Two things, Lydia. First I think she'll appreciate it if you use the word 'lesbian' about her. These days it's not a dirty word though you'd be hard put to believe that on occasions."

"Right. She used it about herself, I think, the word gay I mean."

"Being kind in telling you, I'd guess."

"What was the other thing?"

"Why did you respond with less than enthusiasm?"

"Because of my experience. I do have some knowledge of gays and lesbians…" Deeper darker motives were not to be revealed.

He smiled approvingly. She picked up her knife and fork. "But it's limited to only one episode in my life until now. My late husband, Peter, had a son who was gay and who committed suicide at seventeen. I didn't know Peter at the time. It was the cause of the breakdown of his first marriage. I met him two years after that. When Ellie told me she had met a woman, all I could think of was Gary. I blurted out my – my, not disapproval, honestly Clive, but my concern, yes, concern. I was concerned for her. And then you told me about your partner and what happened. I need to talk."

"It was more a matter of what didn't happen for my partner," he said.

"Exactly. I couldn't bear the thought that Ellie was destined for such misery, or indeed, any misery."

Clive laughed. "I know what you're going to say. She assumed you were prejudiced?"

Relaxed now, Lydia laughed too. "That's right. And her sister did. Polly, my grand-daughter got it right. She saw the parallel with prejudice about older people. But my daughters failed to perceive their own. So were my concerns were justified?"

"Indeed. But you should not have expressed them. She's not a youngster, is she?"

"No. She isn't. But I've got to confess to a slight resentment towards Ellie. We didn't have the freedom her generation has. She was particularly unpleasant about my straying from the accepted path with Peter."

"I'm right there with you."

"Oh, yes, of course! I'll have to apologise to Ellie. Neither of my daughters would speak to me for some weeks, but that's changed a bit now. Kate's in trouble and she came to me." Lydia frowned. "Actually, I think Ellie has a few problems already. Her partner is not well."

"Have you met her, the partner?"

"No, she's a big secret." She paused. "Thanks for listening, Clive. You have cleared my confusion. I see what I have to do. I must apologise to them both before I make the excuses about Peter's son. I so wanted to explain that I was not prejudiced."

"We always want to explain ourselves, don't we?"

"How will they explain themselves, I wonder? Their assumption of my prejudice was a prejudice of their own. How convoluted can relationships get?"

She was thoughtful for a while, accepting that the first thing she must do was to visit Ellie. Kate had said not to visit, but to phone. This sort of dialogue could not be conducted over the phone. She would need to beg to be allowed to visit.

"Clive, any time you need a listening ear, please don't hesitate to ask."

"There is something you can do for me."

"Yes?"

"Come with me to Veronica's funeral. I hate these occasions. False piety, false grief. Dead people suddenly achieve sainthood once they've gone."

"Even Veronica?"

"Even Veronica, a spoiled and selfish woman and she spoiled her son dreadfully. I know a few things about her son."

So did Lydia but she would neither ask nor tell. She also saw Veronica as most people did not. The last meeting with her had been a privilege, the real woman, sad, lonely, guilt-ridden, revealed.

Clive changed the subject. "Are you looking forward to the talk this afternoon?"

"I am. It's a satisfying coincidence that she's doing the talks now, as I'm making big changes in my life."

"The move?"

"Not so much the move. More letting go of the past. I was clinging onto memories of Peter, that was not a good thing and he'd have been appalled. Do you ever try hard to recall things, especially people, and find you can't visualise their faces?"

"I've known that."

"I used to try to visualise Peter and it was as though he'd escaped me. And do you know, letting go of the house, not reliving the memories there, I can see him more clearly now, his kind eyes, his warm smile. He was a lovely man." She gazed wistfully out of the window, down to the milling Friday afternoon crowds on the streets.

"You didn't hear Barbara Wills' first talk, though, did you? Her opening gambit shocked a lot of people."

"What did she say?"

"No one gets out of this life alive!"

On the way home to Tarascon Court with Clive, Lydia saw, ahead of them, Polly, with a boy, obviously Jez. They were holding hands. A terrible sadness came over her as she watched them. In a split second, she was looking ahead, seeing the future for Polly, the pain, the triumph, the maturing, the regrets and at the same time, she saw herself at the same age, some fifty-five years ago, innocent, optimistic. And, for her, all those adventures were over and she was on her own. Not much changes, really, despite smart phones, electric cars and solar panels and, yes, same-sex marriage.

* * *

Lydia was inspired. That evening she phoned Polly to suggest she brought Jez round for tea at Tarascon Court on Saturday afternoon.

"I wondered if you'd like to come shopping with me in the morning?"

"Tomorrow? In the morning?" said Polly. "Are you buying more curtains or something else for the flat?"

"No. I'm choosing the menu for your tea later, with Jez. I thought you'd like to help me. You'll know what Jez likes. I know nothing about the finer points of burgers."

"Finer points of burgers?" Polly spluttered and Lydia could tell she was not at home alone. "Are there finer points to them?"

"I don't know, you see. Are you at home? You can tell Mum you'll be out for lunch, too."

"Yes, I'm at home. I'm doing revision. With Jez."

Many things, Lydia reflected, those sort of indulgences had been called, but revision was a new one.

"In the dining room," Polly added, laughing. "I'd love to come shopping with you, Gran, and have lunch with you. That's a lovely idea. Thank you. What time?"

"Ten o'clock? Can you be up that early?"

"Of course I can. Mum will be glad. She's not well. She just mooches about the house. She's off work. I think it's about Nick."

"Nick?"

"Yes, he spends all his time with Rochelle. Even nights."

Once that call ended, Lydia needed to speak to Kate. Kate assured her she was fine, really, having a rest and enormously grateful for Lydia's help on Tuesday.

"Polly is coming to me tomorrow. I told her to tell you. And also, I wanted to ask about Nick. She said he spends all his time with his girl friend."

"Oh, dear. Life is passing me by, I'm so wrapped up in my misery. I forgot to mention it. Yes, that was Wednesday he brought her home. He spends all his time there, at her place. I suppose it's too tense here. A nice girl."

"You've met her, then?"

"She came here. I haven't set eyes on them since. And I hadn't set eyes on Rochelle before then."

"A bit of a surprise, then?"

"Life's like that at the moment, surprises, shocks. Nick and Rochelle plan to go to uni together. He is nearly eighteen, Mum. I'm just relieved she's a responsible and quiet girl."

"I'll be interested to meet this Jez."

"I think he's a decent enough sort. Polly seems very happy, anyway."

Lydia replaced the phone. That was all she needed to

confirm her loneliness, Polly pre-occupied with a boy-friend.

At ten o'clock on Saturday morning, Polly arrived at Tarascon Court. Here was a new Polly, with long, flowing hair, a long skirt and a loose top. The heavy make-up was gone, her eyebrows defined only by judicious tweaking.

"Now," said Lydia as they walked into town, "about these burgers. I'm not too happy about them."

At the supermarket, the one where Dan worked, Lydia was left to make decisions about the tea party, and bought some smoked salmon, a salad, and scones and a sponge cake. Polly, with no burgers, followed her grandmother around until not long before three o'clock when she went to meet Jez.

Lydia stood at the window, watching and waiting for them. She saw them, walking along the road hand-in-hand, swinging their arms between them. Even from a distance she could see they were engrossed in each other. She watched them, envying them their youth, nostalgic for hers. Polly was growing up, and away, from her.

Lydia opened her front door. There was Polly, all pink and giggly, with Jez. Introductions were made.

"I've heard all about you," Jez said to Lydia. "Polly is always talking about you."

He was tall, fair and not especially good-looking but genial and clearly adored Polly. They all sat at the little table in the window for tea, looking down on the road, the car park and across the water-meadows to the wooded hills beyond. The talk was full of banal jokes to cover-up for the awkwardness of Polly and Jez. Lydia asked him where he lived.

"Not far from us," Polly said..

"By the park," Jez said.

"We meet up in the in the park," Polly added. "In the bandstand. There are a few of us, aren't there, Jez?"

Jez replied. "There's Daz, Baz, Greg and Val. She's a girl. Not from our school though, is she, Polly?"

"She was a goth. But she's not now. I tried it but I don't suit black. Not that I had many black clothes. And Mum went spare, anyway, especially when I wanted to dye my hair black." She leaned forward to peer out of the window. "That car. That yellow one. It's Mr Hornby's. I know it is."

"He's left our school," Jez said.

"He's gone to Mum's school. The little kids. He gives Mum a lift home every evening. At least, he did before she was off sick."

"Is she a bit better?" Lydia said.

"It's doing her good, not going to work. She is calmer. And she's been to see you, hasn't she, Gran? It's all mended now, isn't it?"

"It is," Lydia said.

"I want to go to say 'hello' to Mr Hornby."

"I'd rather you didn't."

Polly stared. "Why not? He's just come in. I know where the flat is."

"Polly, no. You have a guest here. Anyway, his mother's just died. He won't want to be bothering with you."

"His mother has just died? Poor Mr Hornby. I could tell him how sorry I am."

"No."

"Aw! Jez knows him, too, don't you, Jez?"

"I had a disagreement with him," Lydia said.

Polly's turned big eyes to her. "I hope you don't fall out with everyone," she said. She sat back in her chair, her expression the beginning of a pout.

"Tell Gran about your Mum," she said to Jez.

"My mother is Dutch," he said. "She comes from The Hague. We go there every year. She used to be a nurse, but now she teaches sex-education to teachers. My dad scarpered years ago."

Safe sex, Lydia thought. Polly had wanted her to know she was safe. There was no real reason to talk Polly out of having a boy-friend. Not that she would have attempted to do so, but the wish had to be abandoned.

Jez visited the bathroom, giving Lydia the chance to speak to Polly. "He's a really nice young man. I'm a bit disappointed in you and your behaviour this afternoon."

"Well…why can't I go and see Mr Hornby?"

"Polly, please don't keep on about Mr Hornby. The answer is 'no'."

"If you keep on saying I can't see him, I'll leave."

"If you go on like this, I will ask you to," Lydia said. She knew she was risking the relationship with Polly, but there was no other way of dealing with this request. A long silence followed.

"Really? What about Jez?" Polly said last.

"What about me?" he said coming back into the room.

Polly put her elbows forcibly onto the table and leaned her face on her hands. "Gran's nagging me."

"If it's still about Mr Hornby, I don't know why you bother. He's a geek."

"Oh!" Polly stood, pushing her chair back roughly. "I'm going to see Mr Hornby if *you* are turning against me."

"I'm not turning against you."

"You'll do nothing of the sort, Polly. I don't want you to have anything to do with that man."

Polly sat down again. "Why not? He's friends with Mum. She approves of him. He gives her a lift home after school every day."

"I don't trust him. Now finish your tea. You're embarrassing Jez."

"No, I'm not."

"Yes, you are," Jez said.

Polly stared at him.

"And," he continued, "I think you and I should have a private chat about this, when we leave here. I'm sure your Gran has reason for not wanting you to speak to Mr Hornby."

"Finish your tea," Lydia said.

They all sat in silence for what seemed a long while. Tea was finished. Jez rose to his feet again.

"Mrs Grover," he said, "it's been a lovely tea and thank you very much for inviting me. I've enjoyed meeting you. But I think we should go now, me and Polly. My Mum always says that if you have a disagreement with someone, it's best to talk about it."

He held his hand out to Lydia. "I'm sorry, Mrs Grover."

Lydia stood and took his hand. "I think your mother's advice is very sound."

The stunned Polly gazed up at him then at Lydia. "Now see what you've done!" she burst out.

"I haven't done anything."

"I only wanted to see Mr Hornby."

"I only wanted you not to see him." Lydia peered out of the window. "He's gone, now, anyway."

Polly leaned to peer out of the window. Below, the yellow car was leaving Tarascon Court. She sat down on her chair and burst into tears.

"I'll wait for you downstairs," Jez said.

"I don't know how you can let this happen, Polly," Lydia said as Jez left. "He's a decent boy. He reminded me of Peter. He has his qualities. I'm envying you. I'm sad to be on my own, and you are wasting him."

Polly did not reply. She stood up, went to the door, took her jacket and slammed out of the flat.

Lydia phoned Kate after clearing away the remains of the tea party. Kate must have been more familiar with Polly's adolescent tantrums. She was hardly bothered.

"Mum, can I pop round to see you? In the morning? Half-ten-ish?"

Again? Lydia swayed between triumph and anxiety. "I'll wait for you downstairs," she said, "in the hallway. I'll prepare us a light lunch and you can sit and do nothing but gaze at the view."

"I can't bear being alone at the moment. I don't like me very much."

"I love you, Kate, you are one of my babies, my first one."

Keeping watch from her living room window on Sunday morning, Lydia spied her daughter's slouching body coming into view. Thank God Kate was in touch again. The family had to be juggled. Only one was able to be kept in touch at any one time. Now it was Kate, once it was Polly, but not any more. She hurried down in the lift and was waiting with the front door open as Kate approached.

"Come on in and be made a fuss of," Lydia said, hugging her.

"Thanks, Mum," Kate murmured. They both turned to go to the lift. Next to her, Lydia felt Kate go rigid. She glanced in the direction of Kate's fixed stare. Coming down the staircase was Ashton Hornby. He walked straight towards them.

"Mum...," Kate said.

"His car's not there," Lydia said.

"Well, well, well," he said, a triumphant smile on his face. "Mother and daughter, is it? Well, well, well."

Lydia tried to urge Kate to the lift, but Kate was frozen, staring at the man.

"I've got to say," and he was addressing Kate, "your mother was the better lay."

Kate looked stunned for a few seconds. A snarling noise came from her. She lunged forward, her fists flailing, pummelling him blindly. Her right hand opened and she drew her nails down his left cheek, then grabbed his shirt and tie, pulling buttons off the shirt.

Lydia made futile efforts to pull her away. He managed to grab Kate by the wrists, wrenched her hands away from him, holding her arms far apart and twisted, on either side of her body.

"I'll go to the police about this," he hissed.

"Why don't you?" Lydia's calm voice caught the attention of both Kate and Ashton. "They would be interested to hear your stories, along with those of Cathy and Cathy's sister. Not to mention, my story and Kate's. You're a bastard. Your mother was ill and you neglected her. But you're always here now, plundering her flat."

"That's your opinion. Who's going to believe a couple of bitter women?"

Kate was released. She doubled over, nursing her

bruised wrists. Ashton charged out of the main door. Lydia watched him go, before she led Kate to the lift.

Upstairs in the sanctuary of the flat, Kate fell onto the sofa, her face covered by her hands. In silence, Lydia applied cream to the bruises on her daughter's swelling wrists. After a while, Kate spoke from behind her hands.

"Who's Cathy?"

"My next-door neighbour."

"Her sister?"

"In London."

"That's where he was before."

"I know."

"I feel an idiot. Naive. Made a fool of."

"Don't. No need."

"Tell me it was a lie."

"It was a lie, Kate. But only just. I came to my senses just in time."

Lydia was standing at the window. Ashton Hornby marched along the road. How she would cope with Veronica's funeral on Friday she didn't know. She would have to go. Letting Clive down was out of the question. Fervently, she hoped that that would be the last she would see of Ashton Hornby.

"That man has caused so much trouble," she said. "He was the unlikely cause of Polly's and my difference of opinion yesterday."

"Ashton Hornby was? How?"

"He was here yesterday afternoon and she wanted to go to see him. I said no."

But Kate was not interested in that, or she had no mental space for such trivia.

"I'll make some coffee," Lydia said.

"But, _you?_ How could you?" Kate wailed. "How could you? You're nearly twice his age. Did he not know you're my mother? I've been working with him for weeks."

Kate stretched herself out on the sofa. Lydia made the coffee. She fetched a throw to drape over Kate. She stooped to her and spoke softly.

"Listen, Kate. He is a man of no principles. I've watched him coming and going since Veronica died, taking her stuff. While she was alive, he rarely visited and if he did, it wasn't for long. He uses people, he conquers women. We're not the only ones, believe me and what has my age got to do with anything?"

Without opening her eyes Kate said "When?"

There was no doubt about the significance of the question. "Two days after I moved in. The one occasion, only. I don't want you to think about it."

"I bet you don't." Kate's eyes fluttered open. "I don't quite know how to deal with it all."

"You don't have to. There's nothing to deal with. He's very persuasive."

"It's the implication of what he said, the - the comparison…"

"He wants to hurt you and to come between us. He told the lie for that reason, to hurt you and to punish me."

"He's done more than that. He's devastated me."

"He's leaving. He won't be teaching here any longer. He's going back to London. Cathy told me."

"More choice there."

"The flat belongs to him, Veronica's flat. He doesn't have to wait for his inheritance. It's his and it's on the market now."

Kate's eyes were wide open. "I can go back to my

139

job? Oh, what a relief." She sat up and looked around. "Can I have that coffee now? I want to tell you what's been happening at home."

"Tell me," Lydia said.

Kate followed her to the kitchen. "Well, it's Dan. He's getting on my nerves. He spends money like it's water, he thinks it doesn't matter. The atmosphere is terrible and Nick has all but left home."

"Polly said. Where's he gone?"

"To his girl-friend. Her mother is on her own. She's quite happy to have him. He's moaning about the atmosphere at home and Polly is a pain."

"Nick has actually gone?"

"More or less. They plan to go to uni together. I haven't got the energy to deal with it, so I don't argue. Dan is furious. Mum, I'm planning to leave him."

"To leave Dan?"

"Yes. We just don't get on."

"Were you thinking like this before, you know...?"

"Not exactly. But I realise I can't stay now."

"Where will you go?"

"Dan's all for selling up. Renting, he suggested. He thinks we can repay our debts that way."

"There wouldn't be enough money to purchase two flats, though, would there? Speak to Ryan, at the estate agents'."

"Peter's estate agency?" Kate shrugged. "I don't know."

"It sounds as though things are ripe for a change."

"That's because you've made a big change, that's why you say that. You've done it, haven't you?"

Lydia started at the phrase. "What? Moved, you mean?"

Kate actually laughed. "Moved, yes. Mum, aren't you a bit old for that sort of caper?"

"You're referring to *him* now? Kate, as you age, you realise things don't disappear. Change, yes, but not disappear. Older people still have feelings, you know. We all still function."

"Then I needn't be in a hurry." Kate laughed again, a brief laugh but her face was transformed. "Polly says you have a boy-friend," she said, joining Lydia at the table in the window to drink her coffee.

"Why does she say that?"

"She saw you. Last Friday. It wasn't…?"

"Last Friday? In the afternoon? That would be Clive." It was her turn to be amused. "We go to the talks at the church hall. Ageing. *The Wise Side of Life*, it's called. Don't get any ideas about Clive. He's gay."

"Mum…"

Lydia waited.

"I've been so lonely."

"I know, dear. I have been, too. I think it's a feeling you have to accept. No one is going to be your saviour. It's wrong to rely on other people to sort out your problems. It's using them."

"Where did you get that idea from?"

"Friday afternoons with Clive. It's not loneliness, really I think."

"What is it, then?"

"I don't know until next Friday afternoon."

* * *

"I am alone," Barbara Wills said, moving around the church hall to make sure everyone heard her every word. "But that does not mean I am lonely."

It was Friday afternoon at the talk on *The Wise Side of*

141

Life. Barbara Wills went on to explain the difference between being alone and loneliness. Lydia was not comfortable with what she was hearing. "You can be alone in a crowd. You can choose to relate to those around you. Or you can feel lonely, abandoned, isolated. Being alone can be enjoyable. Being lonely is miserable and usually means you feel the need of people to lean on or rely on."

"I've been lonely and alone," she said to Clive at the tea break. "I still am, in a way. I've had this dreadful confrontation with my grand-daughter and I'm just so sorry about it. I miss her so much."

"I thought it was your daughters who were the problem."

Lydia took a sip of tea, aware of his amusement. "It was. Kate is fine now. But Polly isn't." Polly's words, *'I hope you don't fall out with everyone'*, rose up from a part of the depths of her mind that liked to bother her.

"Sounds like a typical family," Clive said. "Thank God I never had one."

"Don't tell me you and Nigel never rowed."

"Oh, we did. We had such high expectations of each other, made such demands on each other."

"Is that what I'm doing? With my family?"

"Only you will know. With me and Nigel, it was always, each of us wanting the other to do, to be, the impossible. In the end he had to wrestle with his own demons and I with mine."

She looked at him as she wrestled with hers, needing the daughters, needing Polly, despite her lectures to herself.

"Have you been listening to Barbara?"

"Yes. Well, when I wasn't trying to apply some of it to myself."

"It's like the choir," he said. "We're all individuals. Some of us have never spoken to a good few others. Yet, when we are singing, we are united, we are as one. Life's like that. You don't need to own other people. We are all in it together anyway. I'd say you're trying too hard, Lydia. We're all alone, yet, because of that we are all together."

Then she said it. "I don't want to die alone."

"That's what Barbara said where all afraid of. And we are all trying to control what happens after our last breath, too. Damn it, Lydia, don't start crying, not here, for God's sake."

"You seem to cope so well," she said, dabbing her eyes.

"No, I don't. We're all in it together."

She told him about last Saturday's teatime scene with Polly and Jez and how Jez had left. She told him that, after seeing Kate on Sunday, there had been silence ever since.

"I'm afraid to phone. I want to hear that Polly and Jez are still together. They were such a lovely young couple. I so envied them. It took me back to when I was their age and had my first boyfriend. It was all so sweet and innocent, then, I remember. He was lovely, too."

"I doubt your grand-daughter and her boy-friend are as sweet and innocent as you were with your first love. It's all far from innocent these days."

Lydia registered the dismay that rose in her. There it was again, that need to control someone, Polly this time. For one moment, she had the shocking regret that she had resisted the opportunity Ashton Hornby had offered her. All of this, she thought, glancing round the troubled assembly, all of this and sexual jealousy, too. She had never felt so alone, not even after Peter had died.

"Clive, I think I'll go back home now. I need to sort myself out."

Now, even Clive's friendship was posing a problem for her. Was she beginning, oh, so very slightly, to fall in love with him?

* * *

"They're like black crows around road kill," Clive observed as Lydia joined him at the window on the fifth floor landing. They watched the black–clothed residents of Tarascon Court assemble on the forecourt of the flats. It was the day of Veronica's funeral, a dismal March day, with gusts of wind and rain that was heavy at times.

"Isn't that a bit heartless?" Lydia said.

"No more than the chief mourner is," he said. "All charm, smiles and soft words, but a heart as hard as nails." He turned to smile at Lydia. "Thanks for accompanying me to this hypocritical charade. Take no notice of me. I'm only bitter because I don't have a doting mother to bury."

"What happened to her, your mother?"

"Cut me off without a penny."

Lydia thought of her broken relationship with Ellie, and with Polly whom she had not heard from either. Could she risk some sort of approach to Ellie soon? The dilemma was between appearing too eager, too intrusive and of giving the impression of not caring.

"How can a mother turn against her offspring? I find

it hard that my daughter thinks I could do that for the reason she seems to believe."

She and Clive joined the waiting residents outside the main entrance. Clive produced a large black umbrella to shelter them both from the rain. The hearse drew up, laden with wreaths, the largest in white at the side of the coffin reading "MOTHER".

"He neglected her," Clive muttered.

Ashton Hornby was visible in the first of the following cars. Lydia turned her face away when he looked in her direction. The procession of mourners, following the hearse on foot from Tarascon Court, made a slow journey round the corner to the church, where a short service was held. Ashton Hornby paid an emotional tribute to his dear , departed mother as he stood by her coffin.

"Look," Clive said, as they filed out of the church, "frightened bunnies, all of them." He nodded towards a group of Veronica's neighbours, who also had not cared much for Veronica, and were standing, white faced, damp-eyed, showing their muted horror at being confronted by death "I think it's disrespectful to a body to destroy it by burning it. Much more natural to let it decay in the ground, and have a place on Mother Earth forever, don't you?"

"That sounds to me like a yearning for some kind of immortality."

"Maybe."

"Peter was cremated. The thought still appals me. But it's the done thing now."

"I've made no arrangements to go to the crematorium with that lot," he said. "Let her be consumed by the flames, her over-indulged, fossilised

145

body. There was little life in her before she died. As for Ashton…"

Lydia did not want to hear about Ashton Hornby. "There won't be many at my funeral," she said.

"It'll be too late," Clive said, with a laugh, "to be measuring your popularity then."

"It's not that so much. I'm recognising that I have neglected to make friends. Peter and I were sufficient for each other. I didn't feel the need for friends. It was wonderful while he was alive, but afterwards…" She allowed her silence to tell the story. "I've been so lonely," she continued. "I know Veronica was a sad character, turned in on herself, but she was the first friend I'd made for years. I knew her vaguely some time ago, but recently she taught me to be a friend. I'm grateful to her for that. Now I have you as a friend, and Cathy, and am gaining confidence in meeting new people. When it comes to loneliness, I am an expert on that, Clive."

"Barbara Wills has more to say on that subject at the next talk," Clive said. "Thank you for the compliment of thinking of me as a friend. Shall we go for a coffee at Claire's Tea Rooms?"

As they entered the tearooms Lydia saw a familiar figure sitting at a table in the window. It was Rosemary, the bus driver.

Rosemary waved as Lydia approached, her face all smiles.

"Here is another potential friend," Lydia said to Clive. "She rescued me when I had a bad turn on the bus."

"Lydia!" Rosemary greeted her. "How are you?"

"I feel great, thanks. How are you?"

Rosemary nursed her cup of coffee with both hands. "I'm making progress. I took my own advice. The advice I gave you."

"It works?"

"It's working. But I'm not there yet. Not yet. I'm not going back on the buses, either."

"Rosemary, I have a friend with me…"

"So I see." Rosemary gave a cheerful laugh.

"But do keep on with your efforts. I've never forgotten your help and advice. Could we meet up here, perhaps, and exchange ideas?"

"I'd say 'yes'," Rosemary said, "but I'm away over the next weeks. Easter, you see. Could you remember an arrangement for three weeks' time?"

"Three weeks today? Yes, of course. What time? Shall we say half-past ten?"

"Yes! The rain might have stopped by then!"

Lydia rejoined Clive at a corner table.

"You were kind to her," he said as they sat down. "What's the story?"

Lydia recounted the events on the evening of the family lunch party and how Rosemary had been not only kind but efficient.

"You're making up for lost time," he said, "making friends."

They ordered coffee.

"Here's to Veronica," he said, lifting his cup. "And the lessons difficult people can teach us."

Lydia laughed. "Veronica," she said and to herself observed that the encounter with Veronica's son was not all bad because it had reawakened in her a desire for close physical contact which she had neglected in recent years. She would encourage Kate to try to see her experience like that, if only she knew how to approach such a doubly delicate matter.

* * *

She was doing it all wrong, losing her nerve. There was something distasteful about chalking up, in her mind, her friends. Perhaps the move had been all wrong, she should have stayed in the house, with her memories. Being there, she would have had a purpose in life, looking after it, enjoying it. All she had was a small flat. The truth was she still had not got a life.

And now there was a complication about Clive.

Lydia's hand hovered over her phone which was lying on the table. She took a deep breath, picked it up. She knew Ellie's number by heart, even after all these weeks. The ring tone was loud and clear before it switched to an answering service. She cut off the call. What a relief, Ellie was not at home or was busy and had switched off her phone.

The rain continued for several days, even lasting to the following Friday and the afternoon of Barbara Wills' last talk on *The Wise Side of Life*. It was a pithy talk, a final desperate call to her audience to take note of the message.

"You are not merely trying to avoid being alone," she said. "You're filling space and time, using people to rescue you from the task of facing the most important part of your life. You are not lonely, you're not alone. You are afraid, afraid of the truth, the ultimate fact which, if faced up to, will give meaning and shape and purpose to your life at this age."

Was this, Lydia forced herself to think, what she was

still doing, still yearning for Ellie and for Polly and clinging to Kate and her problems to give meaning to her life when it had its own meaning? She glanced at Clive, reluctant to indulge in another deep conversation with him.

"Do you know," he said, "I'm quite relieved to realise that when I die, there will be no one to miss me as I missed Nigel. There will be no one holding on to me and no one for me to hold onto."

"It's as bad as trying to look younger than your age," Barbara Wills was saying with regard to clinging to people. "Accept it, your ageing, with all its wonders!"

"Well, I don't try to do that," Lydia muttered to Clive, "try to look younger. I can't be bothered."

"For my parting comment," Barbara Wills boomed in triumph, "let me quote Rilke: *'we need, in life, to practice only this: letting each other go. For holding on comes easily: we do not need to learn it.'*"

"Who's Rilke?" Lydia said.

"A poet," Clive said. "Foreign bloke. No need to take any notice of him." He chuckled.

Lydia was anxious to reach home. Clive's company was beginning to be a source of unease. The words of Barbara Wills were anything but a comfort. Since before the move, she had put a lot of effort into trying to "get a life" as Polly had put it. She had moved, lightened her load of possessions and responsibilities. She was trying not to rely on her daughters and grandchildren in a clinging and claiming manner. All she had achieved was to have alienated them.

From the depths of her handbag, her phone rang as she let herself in her front door. She fished for it blindly as she turned the key in the lock.

It was Polly calling. There had been no word from her since the tea party with Jez.

"Polly?"

"Gran?" There was a whine in Polly's voice.

"Yes? What is it? You sound upset."

"Is Mum with you?"

"Here, you mean? No, dear. Why?"

"Gran, I can't open the bathroom door. I don't know where she is. I'm scared it's her that's stopping the door opening. It's like she's lying against it."

A stab of fear left Lydia breathless. "I'll come round right away," she said. "In the meantime, can you phone Ellie? She's nearer."

"She's away. I phoned Nick. I tried Mum's phone but there's no answer. She's switched it off, wherever she is."

"I'm on my way. Try not to worry. See if you can find her coat and shoes."

Lydia rushed from Tarascon Court. All other concerns were wiped from her mind as she fought to obliterate the question: had Kate done something silly?

She arrived at Alexandra Street, her heart pounding as much from anxiety as from her haste.

Polly's tear-stained face peered round the door.

"Hurry, Gran, hurry."

"How long have you been home from school?"

"I dunno."

Lydia did her best to race up the stairs. When she reached the top, her legs were weak and she needed to get her breath. She tried the bathroom door.

"See?" Polly said.

Lydia shoved the door hard, leaning her shoulder against it, wincing on the impact. The door gave less than an inch. She made another attempt.

"Don't!" Polly cried. "You'll have a heart attack."

Despite protests from Polly, she tried once more. There was a crunching noise as the door moved at last. "I don't think it's Kate behind there. It feels sort of crunchy."

"Is it her bones?" Polly shrieked.

"No, it isn't. It's the ceiling come down. It's plaster."

"The ceiling?"

"That's right." Lydia had to get her breath. She lowered herself gently to sit on the stairs. "It's not your Mum. It's all this rain. There must be a slipped slate on the roof. It's let the rain in and that's made the plaster soft."

Downstairs, the lock of the front door grated and the door slammed.

"Polly!" Nick called. He began to ascend the stairs in great leaps, pausing when he reached Lydia. "What are you doing here?"

"The same as you," Lydia said, refusing to dwell on him or his response to her.

"Gran says it's not Mum, it's the ceiling come down," Polly said.

"Thank God for that," he said.

"She's hurt herself, look, Gran has." She indicated Lydia rubbing her painful shoulder. "Can you push it wide open, Nick? I'm waiting for a wee."

Nick stepped over and round Lydia. At the bathroom door, he threw his whole body weight against the door. It flew open and he went in with it, staggering amongst the debris of plaster and sodden insulation material. He stooped to move some of it.

"Don't touch it. You'll be itching like mad," Lydia told him as she hauled herself to her feet.

"How do you know?" he said. He avoided eye contact with her.

"Experience," she said. "And you only owe me an apology. I haven't forgotten."

He gave a startled glance and she knew this was because he was used to his grandmother being all sweetness and light. Barbara Wills' words, the whole message, had struck a deep chord within her. There was to be no more dancing around members of the family because she needed their goodwill. She would welcome it, the goodwill, but would not demonstrate her need for it.

"You owe Ellie an apology," he said.

"That's between me and Ellie. This is between you and me."

"You deserve what I said."

"I may have deserved the rebuke but not the insult."

"Are you still in a bad mood?" Polly said after she and Nick had exchanged raised eyebrows.

"It's not a mood, Polly. I'm getting a life." She longed to ask if Polly had made it up with Jez and was getting her own life, but considered it best to refrain from such a question.

Down in the hall, the front door opened again.

"Mum!" Polly pushed her way past Lydia and Nick to fly down the stairs to Kate who was standing in a wet raincoat that dripped puddles onto the tiled floor.

"Mum?" Kate said, gazing up to Lydia on the landing.

"The ceiling's come down," Nick said. "In the bathroom."

Kate stood at the foot of the stairs, her face had gone white. "Oh, no! That's all I needed," she said.

Lydia, nursing her right arm and shoulder, made careful progress down the stairs.

"I thought you were hurt behind the bathroom door," Polly told Kate. "Gran came in a panic."

Kate put out a helping hand to Lydia. "You've hurt yourself, Mum. You look a bit pale. Come and sit down."

In the sitting room, Lydia lowered herself, with difficulty, into the usual chair. She noticed the Royal Worcester dinner set, tucked in the corner, in its box, opened but hardly unpacked.

"Nick!" Kate called.

"What?" Nick drawled from upstairs.

"Kate, don't let him speak to you like that. It's awful."

"Nick, come here, please."

He took his time before he appeared in the doorway.

"Please don't speak to me like that, Nick. Now, will you go and make tea for everyone? Your Gran looks the worse for wear and I feel worse for wear."

He went without a word.

"I thought it was you, behind the door, Kate. I thought – oh, I don't know what I thought."

"Mum, things are bad. Even worse now because of the ceiling. But not that bad. Honestly."

"No. Of course not. I'm glad. I tried to phone in Ellie a couple of times. You said it was best to phone her. But there was no answer."

"They're away, Ellie and Rosie. In Australia. Rosie has family out there, Sydney. Ellie wants to see you when she comes back. She phoned last night."

"Australia? That's a long way to go for a holiday."

"Yes. They're thinking of moving out there."

Lydia sat in the chair, crumpled and dazed. Her shoulder was painful, her mind swirling. Kate was expressing her opinions of Dan's incompetence in managing the house, Nick offered tea. He might also have offered an apology for his behaviour in January, Lydia wasn't sure if it really happened or had she conjured up an apology. No one seemed to appreciate her state of mind.

Australia! It was so shocking, so unexpected, so far.

Polly had made an attempt to clear some of the debris in the bathroom. Through the fog of Australia, Lydia observed that the girl appeared to be happy. She and Jez were making plans for a summer holiday, though exactly where escaped Lydia.

Kate spoke, discreetly, because of the proximity of Nick and Polly, of her increasing desperation to leave Dan.

"I've been at school all afternoon, talking to the Head. She was really kind. And I'm going back at the beginning of the summer term. In a couple of weeks."

"Good," Lydia said, dragging the word from beneath her preoccupation with Australia.

Polly appeared, which hindered Kate's confidences. "Ellie is going to Australia," she said. "I'd like to do that."

"I feel like I'd like to run miles," Kate said. "I don't care where to, I just feel a complete failure."

"You should get a qualification." Lydia ground out the words. It was an effort but she didn't want to hear Kate, too, voicing any ambitions to go to Australia.

"How, Mum? How would the roof and the ceiling in

the bathroom be paid for if I took myself off on some training course?" She hesitated as she saw Lydia flinch.

"Is your shoulder hurting? Sorry, Mum. I came in so buoyed up by my chat with the Head and I came down with a bump when I realised about the ceiling. And you, thinking it was me, behind the door... I should have taken more notice."

This concern could have moved Lydia, but everything she heard, saw, experienced, was through a great barrier. A Great Barrier Reef, she thought. Her own.

Unable to concentrate any more, she made the excuse that her shoulder was painful and she would like to go home.

Polly walked with her for some of the way. So, everyone was fine, Polly with Jez, talking about their problems and preparing for GCSE's ahead of them, Nick planning to go to Uni with Rochelle, after A levels, to study maths, was it? Kate was plotting her way out of the marriage, Ellie off to Australia with Rosie. And for herself? Her biggest fear was going to be realised, eventually, the one she had never really faced, the possibility that she would die alone.

* * *

Late one afternoon, Lydia had an unexpected caller. It was Dan.

"On your own?" she asked over the entry-phone.

"Yes, I'm on my way home from work. I had an early shift today."

She let him in, not surprised at this visit, but disappointed that he was alone. He arrived on the fifth floor, all bon-homie.

"Hello, Lydia. How are you? What a relief the rain has stopped at last. Quite a nice day now, isn't it?"

She indicated the sofa for him and she sat in her own chair. She waited.

"Ellie is back home tomorrow, I think," he went on. "It would be a poor welcome if it was wet like it was last week, after Australia, you know."

"Was there something important to tell me?" she said. Once she would have been welcoming and eager to please because she had vested interests in keeping on the right side of him and in him keeping on the right side of her. But now, she had faced those interests and seen how they warped life and relationships. And anyhow, she didn't like Dan very much. No wonder Kate was exasperated by him. His whole manner was like her manner had been in the past, anxious to please, wanting something.

"Yes, Lydia. I'd been wondering if you could help me, us, I mean."

She didn't make it easy for him. The man wanted money, let him work at asking her. In the past, she'd begged her daughters to allow her to help, financially and in other ways. That attitude she could now see in a different light.

"Of course," she said. "Tell me how I can help."

"You could help if you lent us some money for the roof repairs and the ceiling of the bathroom. I hesitate to ask you, you know, but you must have a comfortable bit stashed away after selling your house."

"I had a comfortable bit stashed away before I sold my house. Peter left me money. Estate agents did well."

"Oh. I didn't know."

Really? "So how much is this work going to cost?"

156

"I don't know."

"You haven't had any estimates done?"

"Not yet."

"I suggest you organise that right away. Then come back to me, with Kate."

"I didn't want to bother her."

"I think you'll find she's already bothered. When you get back, ask her to phone me."

He thanked her even though she had done nothing yet. He left, she mentally dusted him off and smiled to herself.

Kate phoned, it must have been as soon as Dan had given him her message.

"Dan's been round to you, hasn't he, Mum? Asking for money. I didn't know, honestly."

"It's alright, Kate. Can you pop round early tomorrow?"

Kate could, and she did. She was looking much better, almost happy. There was energy about her.

"Is this about money, Mum? He has a cheek. How does he think he's going to pay it back? Because it would have been up to him. I want to leave him. I want to take Polly and rent a flat or something somewhere."

"Does Dan know this?"

"No, I haven't told him, not in the 'sitting–down-this–is–serious way'. I have shouted at him to bugger off, at times, or said I would. That's all."

Lydia shrugged. "It's nothing to do with me, of course. But you decide what you want. The money is there. For you. Dan still owes me for a little debt on his credit card last Christmas."

"I didn't know that."

"Of course you didn't. But I'm talking big sums

157

now. If you want to get some qualifications or to set yourself up in business, I'm quite happy to fund it. But you'll have to swallow your pride."

"Mum…"

"I'm paying for Polly's school trip to France. I promised her that, ages ago. I expect I'll give her some towards this other holiday with Jez. She'll be sixteen by then, won't she?"

Kate laughed. "Your generation, so – what shall I say?"

"Just don't. Is it right, Dan said Ellie's back tomorrow?" From Australia, she thought, swallowing the lump about to rise in her throat.

"Yes. But don't forget jet lag."

"Of course. Have you met Rosie yet?"

"No." Kate shook her head. "She's a big secret. I keep asking. But all Ellie says is she doesn't want a repetition."

"Of what?"

"You know."

"Oh, dear."

"And they're getting married."

"Ellie and Rosie? Oh." Lydia sighed. "I really am past my sell by date, aren't I? I'll never be needed for baby-sitting again."

"Why not? I might marry again. Ellie or Rosie or both might have children one way or another."

"But I won't be able to go to Australia to babysit." And that came out really bitter.

Kate gazed at her. "Do you feel not wanted? Can you not cast your mind back to when you were my age? Everyone wants me, for everything, all the time."

"That was when I met Peter."

"Count your blessings, Mum. You're free. To do what you want."

* * *

It was the day of the arrangement to meet Rosemary for coffee. Claire's Tea Rooms were all spring-like with tubs of narcissus either side of the door and little vases of violets in the centre of each of the tables. At first, Lydia could not see Rosemary, then from the threshold, she spotted her, sitting in the far corner of the tea room, away from the window. She hurried over, but stopped halfway. Another person was sitting there, next to her, at a round table, a familiar person, whose was face was taut, even anxious, and not her usual golden self. Could it be true? Was it perhaps wishful thinking, her mind playing tricks after all her angst?

"Ellie!" Lydia cried. "Rosemary?"

Rosemary smiled. "I had to talk her into it. She seems to think you were scary. I don't know why." She turned to Ellie.

"Scary? Me? Hello, Ellie." Lydia wanted to cry.

"Mum?" Ellie pushed her chair back, rucking the tablecloth in her nervous haste. She held out her hands. Lydia ignored them, moving round to her to wrap her in a tight hug. She kissed her on her now pink cheek.

"What a wonderful surprise!" Lydia said, standing back to take a good look at her daughter. She turned to the young woman whom she had thought of as Rosemary until now.

"And you have got to be Rosie. And I never realised. Thank you so much for this. How are you?" She leaned towards Rosie and kissed her cheek.

159

"I'm okay. Going on better."

Everyone sat down. Coffee and scones were ordered. An awkward silence ensued.

"How's the flat?" Ellie began.

Lydia put down her cup of coffee and ignored the question to say, "Ellie, I have so missed you."

Ellie took a breath to say something. Lydia shook her head. "No, Ellie, you don't have to explain. I do. I want to apologise to you for my misunderstanding. I really am dreadfully sorry."

Ellie sat, open-mouthed.

"My reaction, when you told us all your news that day," Lydia went on, "must have been extremely hurtful."

Ellie looked down. "It was, but I'm over it now. Please forget it, Mum."

"I want to tell you, both of you, about Peter." The guarded expression that flickered across Ellie's face was undeniable. Lydia swallowed and motored on. She had to do this.

"Peter...?" Ellie said.

"Yes, Ellie. Peter." Lydia turned to Rosie. "I need to tell you both about him. He was my second husband, Rosie. We were married when Ellie was twelve. She did not and still does not approve of him."

"You're right there," said Ellie.

"But I must talk to you about him."

"Go on, then."

That was the best agreement she could hope for from Ellie, Lydia knew. Ellie lowered her eyes.

"Peter had a son, Gary."

"I didn't know that. Did I ever meet him?" Ellie lifted her head.

"No. He died two years before we met. He was gay."

"Oh, I see. Aids."

"No. Suicide. At seventeen."

Ellie gasped. Rosie frowned. It was Rosie who spoke.

"I am so sorry to hear that. It must have been some time ago."

"A long time. Peter never got over it. He had no problem with Gary, except that, at the time, he was under age. But the boy's mother and her family, they could not accept it. This was less than thirty years ago, it was not so readily accepted, not like now. So not only did his mother not like it, the law discriminated and he became so depressed and he ended up taking his life. The atmosphere was different then. There was AIDS panicking everyone, there was 'Clause twenty-eight', a totally different attitude."

"I have a glimmer of how he felt," Rosie said, her eyes brimming with tears. "I have the same problem with my family. They're religious. It seems everything else can be forgiven, except this."

Lydia gazed at her, understanding now her stress and anxiety.

Rosie turned to Ellie. "Your Mum and me, when we met, we spent our conversations giving each other good advice. I've got your name right, now, haven't I? I kept talking about Linda. 'Linda said', I kept saying, didn't I, Ellie? Then Ellie clued in. So I persuaded her to come with me this morning. I hope you don't mind."

"Mind?" It was Lydia who laughed now. "I am so grateful, Rosie, and to you as well, Ellie, dear. I don't suppose for a moment it was easy."

"I didn't sleep," Ellie said. She stirred her coffee vigorously.

"Spring," said Lydia, lifting the posy of violets on the table and savouring their scent. "At last."

Ellie took some sips of coffee before leaning forward to speak to Lydia.

"Mum, how come you know all this about this Gary and you reacted the way you did when I told you?"

"*Because* I knew about Gary. I was concerned about you, being out on a limb, not being accepted and don't forget, I've watched you in the past." She saw Rosie's eyes dart from herself to Ellie. Rosie smiled. Ellie's hand covered Rosie's darker one on the table. Ellie's past was no secret, then.

"Sorry, Mum. I thought it was another example of the ideas of people of your age. And I knew about Rosie's family."

Lydia explained about Clive, his story of his partner. "So, you see, it's not over yet. Clive reckons when our generation has moved on, it'll be different. But will you still be left with other kinds of judgements about people? Polly could see it. The way people of my age are viewed by people of your age."

"I said I'm sorry, Mum…"

"Ellie, it's okay. I'm sorry I was clumsy in what I said. I think the lunch party was a mistake."

"That was Kate, trying to be helpful. You see, I was scared. She knew I was scared, but she didn't know why."

And there was the other, the unspoken assumption on Ellie's part, that Lydia was likely to be unaccepting of Rosie because she was black. They talked for a while about families, Rosie's sister, Lily, about Polly and Jez, her boyfriend, Kate not being well and also having time off work due to stress.

"Would you like to see my flat?" Lydia said as the

energy was running out of the encounter, with coffee and scones devoured. Walking back to Tarascon Court, the conversation was piecemeal but relaxed. Ellie and Rosie talked about their proposed wedding.

"Not until I'm back at work," Rosie said, "or I won't be able to make a financial contribution to the event. And we shouldn't spend too much. It's the marriage that's important, not the wedding."

Lydia agreed and made a mental note to offer financial help when a more suitable moment arose.

"Are you still not working, Rosie?" she asked.

"For a while. I don't want to go back on the buses. You wouldn't believe how nerve-wracking that can be, what with the passengers inside and the traffic outside. Honestly, there's more to worry about than an airline pilot has".

"I'm sure that's true."

"I hope to return to the dance school soon. My pupils will have given up on me soon if I don't."

"You teach dancing?"

"That's how we met. I wanted to learn to dance." Ellie said. "You could learn."

"What sort of dance could I learn?"

"What would you like to learn?" Rosie said.

"Flamenco?"

"Oh, yes. Quite popular."

Lydia laughed. It might be one way towards getting a life.

They were walking across the forecourt of Tarascon Court. Ryan, from the estate agents', emerged from the main doors, accompanied by tall, grey-haired man. Lydia greeted Ryan. Veronica's flat was being sold by Ashton Hornby. Good riddance.

In the kitchen, while Ellie and Rosie admired the flat and were standing arms around each other gazing at the view from the window, Lydia made sandwiches and a phone call to Kate.

"A light lunch and chat," Lydia said.

Kate did not waste time. Ten minutes later, the entry-phone rang to announce her arrival.

"Who's that?" Ellie said, sharpness in her voice.

"Kate. I thought it would be a good idea to ask her too."

"I haven't met Kate," Rosie said. "In fact, I haven't met anyone except you. I've heard about them." She glanced at Ellie. "I've been a big secret, haven't I?"

Lydia watched them. Having seen herself as cast out of the family since the lunch party, she had been sure Kate had been introduced to Rosie.

"Can you blame me?" Ellie said.

"Lydia is no problem," Rosie said, "not for any reason."

Lydia answered the door to a breathless Kate.

"You look better," she said to her.

"I think I am," Kate said and proceeded to step to the living room doorway where she paused.

Rosie came forward, her hand outstretched. "I'm Rosie, the biggest a secret in the West."

"I'm Ellie's sister," Kate said. "I'm really so glad to meet you at last. I've heard so much about you".

Lydia watched Kate, who was disguising any surprise she might be experiencing on meeting Rosie for the first time. The tension on Ellie's face confirmed that Rosie had indeed been a secret, all aspects of her. Like Kate had probably also expected, Lydia had feared that Rosie might be weighty, with her hair cut short, piercings everywhere, brutal-looking, the latter being more than an expectation, but an assumption.

"All good, I hope," Rosie was saying.

"Ellie's happy with you," Kate said. "That's enough for me. I gather that you have not been well. Are you better?"

"Stress," said Rosie, "but on the mend."

"Me, too," said Kate. "Stress, anxiety. Hell."

"In my case, the parents," said Rosie.

"I know what you mean," Kate said and Ellie and Lydia exchanged amused glances, amused for different reasons. "Or perhaps I don't," Kate added.

The four sat around the small, circular table in the window and passed sandwiches to each other. Kate was almost her old self. Rosie explained how she and Lydia had met and subsequently exchanged words of wisdom, not knowing that their relationship was potentially that of mother-in-law and daughter-in-law.

"Dan's got plans to sell the house," Kate said. "I'm not too happy about that." She turned to Rosie. "Me and Dan, we're in debt up to here." She raised her left hand to the level of her nose. "We're drowning in debt."

"I was in debt," Rosie said. "I was doing extra work, on the buses, to catch up. I'd said to Ellie we couldn't possibly be married while I owe money. I'd nearly paid it all off then I got in a state. Overdoing it, you know, didn't I, Ellie?"

"You did. I was so worried," Ellie said. "And you had the extra burden of trying to cope with your parents."

"Have your parents explained their objections?" Lydia asked.

165

"No, not really. But I know. My Dad's religious. So is my Mum but she's not so bad. She has to go along with him, you know."

Lydia gave her attention to Kate. "Selling the house might be the only way," she said.

"Mum was married to an estate agent," Ellie explained.

"Would that have been Peter?" Rosie said.

"It was," Lydia agreed. "Kate, how is Dan?"

"Driving me mad, to tell you the truth. But for a new reason. He's being really pleasant at the moment, taking an interest in things, you know." She stared at her plate. "I think he feels bad about the debt. He spends money without thinking, even now. He wants me to agree to sell. It's not the house so much. It's knowing that once he's got some money, he'll start spending again. Either I let him or I fight." She shrugged. "I don't know what to do." She became tearful. "I feel trapped." She glanced up at her mother, her sister and Rosie. "He feels bad about the debt and he wants me to agree to sell."

Lydia gave Kate an encouraging stroke on her arm. She was thinking, thinking about Kate's problem.

"It's good to see my daughters again. And Rosie, to realise that I knew you all along, too."

"There had been a bit of a stand-off," Kate explained to Rosie. "Between us and Mum."

Rosie smiled, Lydia smiled. *Families,* Lydia remembered, *who needs them?*

"Listen! You know Polly's got a boyfriend?" Kate said. "Well, I found a book hidden under her pillow."

"Porn?" said Ellie.

"No, thank God. Sex education, though. I looked through it, with not too much attention because I felt guilty. But the joke is, it's in Dutch. I think it's Dutch, anyway."

"Could you understand it?" Ellie asked.

"Not the words, except the Latin ones. But the pictures, yes! So explicit. Jez's mother is Dutch. She trains teachers in sex education. I feel reassured about Polly."

There were gales of laughter. Lydia stroked Kate's arm again, to sooth her. Kate was doing well but Lydia felt anxiety on her behalf.

Rosie spoke of returning to work, teaching dance at a studio in the town. She was self-employed, so needed to return. Lydia asked her if she rented the space she used at the studio.

"I do. What I need is a studio of my own so that I can employ other teachers. But unless I go back on the buses, that's never going to happen. My Dad could lend me the money, even give me some, but that's something else that's not going to happen."

"I've got to get back home," Ellie said. "It's all rolling in for me, at the moment. I've got a consultation at three o'clock and another at six." She screwed her face. "Meringues. You know, the dresses? The only day in their lives some girls feel good. They think they are pop stars or acting like a famous person. We'll be a bit more stylish than that for our own wedding, won't we, Rosie?"

"I shall rely on you," said Rosie. "I'd be happy to marry you in rags."

Before they left, Lydia gave Ellie the box she had retrieved from Kate, and another, bigger box that had been stowed in one of the many cupboards in the flat.

"What's in them," Kate whispered as she helped Lydia search the shelves.

"The big one is a Royal Worcester tea service."

"What was in the other one, the one you took back? What did you want out of it?"

"I wanted photos of Gary and a newspaper cutting that I'd put in."

"Can I see?"

"Another time. I'd like to talk to you about money when you're ready."

* * *

There was a bring-and-buy sale being held in the lounge at Tarascon Court. Lydia, having acknowledged that she had been stand-offish with regard to activities there, decided it was time she made an effort to join in. All her instincts fought against it. She was reminded of Veronica's contemptuous attitude towards her neighbours. That woman had been a snob, and so surely, was she, Lydia.

In the process of the move, her new home had been denuded of anything to bring to such a sale. In the end, she snatched a jar of luxury jam from the kitchen cupboard, telling herself to stop the procrastination.

Milling around in the lounge, it was mostly women there. Lydia was noticed straight away, arms reaching out to draw her in.

"Mrs Grover, isn't it?"

"Aren't you on the top floor?"

"How long have you been here?"

"Not long, is it?"

"Come on in. I expect it's taken all this time to get yourself sorted out, has it?"

Lydia smiled grimly to herself. She was not sorted yet. Far from it. And she was not thinking about furniture.

The jam was accepted eagerly from her as though an offering of gold. She was taken to admire two laden tables piled with jams, cakes, trinkets, ornaments and books. She bought a sponge cake to put in her freezer for the next time anyone called.

"It's Lydia Lawrence, surely?" a voice said. "What name are you known by now?"

Lydia turned. "I'm Lydia Grover."

"It's Jennifer, Jennifer North, as was. Remember?"

"Oh, my goodness, I do! Beechfield School?"

"Sh!" said Jennifer. "Don't tell everyone we went to a private school."

"Even after so long?"

"They're mainly from secondary moderns here. And a couple of former grammar school girls. I don't think that the comps have come to retirement age yet. You know, nearly a third of us here are locals. Most of the others come from London…"

Jennifer North, as was, chatted on. She introduced other neighbours including a certain Anne Raynard who had been an irritant neighbour in Lydia's youth, now known as Anne Earnshaw. She had been a rebellious girl, gone off the rails, got herself pregnant in the days when it mattered, and yet here she was, in the same position as Lydia, and was warm and friendly now. What was life about!

Clive popped in, bought Lydia's jam and promised to see her on Wednesday at choir practice. She laughed about the jam.

"I could have given it to you," she said.

He held up the jar. "This isn't jam. This is oil for the social wheels of the neighbours here."

Cathy appeared. "I'm delighted to see you've awoken

169

from your stunned mode after the move," she said. "They have some interesting things going on in here. Some I'm not interested in but you can't do everything, can you?"

Up to now, Lydia thought, she hadn't been able to do anything.

When she returned to her flat, a long while later, with the sponge cake, she was aware of a glow, a sense of well-being. She sat in the sunshine in the big window, enjoying this unfamiliar peace of mind, of enjoyment of simply being. All anxiety about life, about doing the right thing, about all the decisions and changes she had made, seemed to have dissolved. The unforeseen result of all that had happened in recent months was that she experienced a remarkable peace about Peter - at last. She smiled to herself.

The ringing of the entry phone disturbed her. She rose, eagerly. It was Polly.

"Gran! Let me in, please!"

Lydia waited for her by the front door. When the lift doors opened, Polly fell out, rushing towards her, arms held out.

"What's wrong? You're so upset. Tell me." Lydia closed the door, while Polly was still hanging on her arm. It must be Jez. They'd had another falling out, perhaps.

The sobs died down. Lydia took her into the living room. She dabbed the girl's face and wiped her nose as though she was a small child.

"It's Mum. And Dad. Mum told me. They're going to get a divorce."

"I see."

"I don't want them to."

"No, of course not." Lydia waited, her arms round Polly. "Are they arguing then?"

"No." Polly looked up, surprised. "It's past that, I think. They stopped. They've come to an agreement. They - they are going to go their separate ways, Mum said."

"I see. Is it better if Mum's throwing chicken Jalfrezi at Dad, or is it better they don't argue any more?"

Polly looked thoughtful. "You remembered about the chicken Jalfrezi. I was hoping Dad would see everything from Mum's point of view, not just about ready meals, about money, really. Why are they doing this? Mum knows what it's like because you did it to her and you know, too, because my great-grandmother did the same thing. If you and she know how awful it is, why is she doing it to me?"

"It's not a choice, Polly, really. And there could come a time when you find yourself in the same situation as Mum is now, and you will understand how awful *that* is."

"No, never."

"I think sometimes it's a mistake to get married too young."

"What, just have it off with people instead? Is that what you mean?"

Lydia shrugged and kept a straight face. On that, she would not dare to commit herself in case Kate disapproved. Polly grinned then turned away.

"Has Mum, or even Dad, said what their plans are?"

"Mum wants him to go. To leave. She's going to ask you for money for the house, she said. Will you really do that, give her money? I think she's hard. I think it's all wrong."

"Has Dad agreed?"

"I think so. She says she's coming to see you, Mum did."

"Good. How's Jez?"

"Lovely. We talk. Like he said. Mum and Dad should have done that a long time ago. Instead, he just slopes off to avoid trouble, then goes and spends more money."

"I've got a sponge cake in the kitchen. I was going to put it in the freezer but I think we'll have a piece each now, shall we?"

Polly nodded. She followed Lydia to the kitchen. "Will Mum be happier without Dad?"

"In time."

"Will Dad?"

"I would think so."

"Will I?"

"I think that's partly up to you. If you resist the changes and try to make people do what they don't want to do, it will make everyone miserable."

Polly watched her prepare the tea and cut the cake. "That looks nice," she said. "Did you make it or buy it?"

"I bought it. Downstairs." Lydia explained about the 'bring-and-buy' sale and meeting the residents who were old acquaintances, going back to when she had been quite young.

"Oh, that must be really interesting, like going back to school again without the teachers." She took her plate into the living room.

"I met a woman I was at school with and another who was a neighbour. I hated her at the time."

"You hated someone?"

"Anne Maynard. I remember the name so clearly. She's Anne Earnshaw now."

"Earnshaw? Used to live on Gracehill? That's Cordelia's grandmother, her Dad's mother. Oh, Gran, is she horrible?"

"On the contrary, she was extremely pleasant. In fact, I think she made this cake. She lives here, in Tarascon Court."

"Ugh!" Polly feigned disgust as she glanced at the slice of cake. "Oh, well, I suppose people change. There's hope for Cordelia after all."

* * *

It was not all bingo and knitting, though Lydia had attended a couple of bingo sessions. Why had she remained so aloof since she'd arrived at Tarascon Court? she asked herself. In the lounge, a woman named Cynthia, whom she had known in the Brownies, years ago, had organised showing her DVD of the film 'Quartet'. Lydia emerged, blinking and uplifted by a story of a home for retired musicians that painted ageing as enjoyable, romantic, even.

"Mum!"

A familiar voice called her. Across the entrance hall, Kate jumped up from a seat.

"I waited. They said you were watching a film." There was a sense of urgency about Kate, despite her casual tone.

Once in the flat, Lydia tried to gauge her daughter's mood. "Shall I make a cup of tea?"

Kate shook her head.

"Drink, then?"

Again Kate shook her head. "I need to talk to you. About Dan. He's agreed to leave. On conditions."

"Which are?"

"He wants me to have the house, with all the work that's needed on it. He wants the mortgage paid off, for my benefit, but not by him. But there's less than seven years left now, so that's not a big deal. And he'll sod off to some fancy woman I didn't even suspect he had." Kate was breathless with anger.

"And how do you feel about that? Do you want to agree?"

"I'm not in a position to agree or not agree. He seems to think you'll cough up and make life easy for him."

"But you want to stay in the house?"

"If I can. It would be a hassle to have to sell it and uproot ourselves. I can't, for one moment, take it for granted that Nick won't do more than pop back home occasionally during the week. He'll need a home to come back to if and when he goes to uni. What can you do for us, Mum?"

"Certainly, I can pay for the repairs to the roof and to the bathroom ceiling. I could pay off the mortgage for you."

A long sigh came from Kate as she leaned back on the sofa. She began to cry quietly.

"Come on, Kate, there's nothing to be upset about."

"Yes, there is. There are lots of reasons, like Polly and Nick being upset, their world turned upside down. Me, I'm a failure, Dan, deceiving me all the while I kept trying and trying to make it work. There's no hope now, I can't keep him. I'm glad I didn't try too hard to fight off temptation, recently. And there's you."

174

"Me?"

"Yes, I've been horrible to you. I'm really sorry, Mum."

"Kate, don't be too harsh on yourself. Just remember, it could be you being treated like that by Polly at some future date."

For a long while, Kate sat silent. She sighed again. "I am so lucky," she said. "What would I have done if you hadn't been able, not to mention willing, to come to my rescue?"

"You'd sell up and rent."

"Dan, he suggested asking you to pay off his debts for him. I mean, what a cheek! He can ask *her* to help with that. I'm sure he's been spending our money on her. He's going to have to make me an allowance for Polly. And if he gets to Uni, Nick will want some help from him."

"Is it all settled, then?"

"With me and him? I guess so, unless he changes his mind. I need to go to a solicitor now. Is it all right if I go to the one who was Peter's friend? I really can't believe I'm doing this."

***

The choir's Easter concert, a performance of Karl Jenkins' 'The Armed Man' was a satisfying success. No one from Lydia's family attended. They never did. It occurred to her that she should have asked either Kate or Ellie, offered to buy tickets for them. None of them knew what the choir did. Kate had asked the question once. The response was, "Songs?" Lydia had given up.

Easter came and went without much celebration.

Dan had departed to his new woman, leaving Kate feeling angry.

"I know it's what I wanted," she told Lydia, "but he's gone so willingly. Thank God I'm back at work. At least that's going well."

No one had wanted to do anything special over the holiday. Ellie and Rosie were quietly planning their wedding, Polly was with Jez when she was not dredging up bitterness about her Dad. Nick was with Rochelle, manliness forbidding any grief about a deserting father.

"Honestly, on top of my A-levels," he said to Lydia. "Good timing, Dad."

"And my GCSE's," Polly claimed.

Lydia, however, had discovered a social life. She had gone 'over the top' with it, almost recklessly, joining in as much as she could of the activities at Tarascon Court as well as other outside activities. She went to a live-streamed opera from Covent Garden at a local cinema, which Derek Marsden, a single resident of the flats who also attended, along with Jennifer, Anne and a quiet woman named June. The competition for single men may well be fierce, and secret, too. Lydia had no such ambitions. Scrabble took place in the lounge three afternoons a week. She joined in that, as well as a quiz night. Sometimes, because of the excitement, the newness of the people and the activities she could not fall asleep easily. Conversations buzzed around in her head. At other times, self-doubt doubt crept in. Surely she was not as likeable, not as good company, as the impressions she received told her she was.

After Easter, the choir resumed rehearsals for the summer concert. Lydia went along with Clive. The poetry meetings also began then, in the church hall attended by the quiet woman named June and in the second week by the new resident of Veronica's flat, or more correctly Ashton Hornby's flat. The new owner was Desmond Bedford, the tall, grey-haired man she had seen being shown round Tarascon Court by Ryan. She was glad that the ghost of Ashton Hornby had finally been laid. She reported this to Kate, who said nothing but her body language spoke at great deal.

"We never see you these days," was all Kate said. "You seem to be enjoying life."

"So will you, before long, Kate."

"Really? Eighteen years so easily discarded? I've forgotten how to enjoy anything."

"I know that feeling. You'll get over it."

That was when Kate said, "You certainly have. You've gone 'over the top' with your activities."

One day early in May, a group of nearly a dozen residents, organised a day trip by coach to Brighton. It was a successful day. The weather was fine, the company great. At one point, as they were all sitting around a large table in a pub, for a meal, laughing uproariously at non-jokes, Lydia wondered how Kate or Ellie might have seen the party if either of them stumbled upon it. She could hear Kate's voice in her mind's ear, "a bunch of tipsy, old ladies, red-faced and desperate for fun, as if that's all there is to life."

Or were they her own thoughts?

She was quiet in her seat on the coach going home. Views of the swelling Downs spread out before her, thick woods crowded into the creases, birds soared and hovered over the fields and folds. Small homes tucked themselves into sheltered spots, larger ones dominated their territory with arrogance. She must have a chat with

Clive. Since the *'Wise Side of Life'* talks had stopped, she had seen less of him. Her feelings about him had become less of a problem to her. Other interests and other people had displaced that to the point where she was exhausted. Yes, she would have a talk with Clive.

When, hot and tired, the coach passengers reached Tarascon Court, one of the women at the front of the coach called out.

"Something's wrong," she said. "Sue's waiting."

"It's not good news," said another.

The coach bounced awkwardly into the car park and pulled up. Everyone crowded forward to see what could be wrong.

"Sue should have been off duty hours ago," said someone from the front of the coach.

They all clambered eagerly off the coach only to hang back when Sue, looking grim, approached them, bearing the bad news.

"It's Clive," she said. "Clive Morris. He's had a heart attack. In the entrance hall. Here."

"Is he - dead?" There was a reluctance with the word from whoever had spoken it.

"Out like a light. He didn't suffer," Sue said.

The coach passengers began to troop indoors, muttering sad clichés.

"No problems with the stretcher, then," quipped an insensitive resident.

Lydia stood there, in front of the building, in a daze. She was angry at the joke, angry that no one seemed to care much, angry with Clive. She was the last one indoors. She sat on a seat in the entrance hall, her head racing with thoughts. Clive. How could he die, just like that, while she was out enjoying herself? He could have waited, at least until she got home. Now she wouldn't be able to have a chat with him, the chat about balance in her social life. Though he did seem to have put the brakes on that, most effectively. And he had been right about not having anyone grieving over him. Well, nearly right, at least, no one special left behind, only herself. He had gone to Nigel.

The entrance hall was empty now. She supposed she ought to make her way up to her flat. But not yet. She needed a moment more to recover.

The lift doors parted. She gasped. Out stepped a figure. She thought it was Clive. For one moment it was as though the homecoming had been an unpleasant dream, until she recognised it was Desmond Bedford, the new owner of number nineteen, Veronica's flat. He was wearing a Bowls Club blazer.

He came towards her.

"I thought you were Clive," she said. "You're wearing his blazer."

"The Bowls Club," he said. "Bad news about him, eh?"

"Yes. Very sad. He was kind to me. Oh, dear, look at me. I'm shaking." She lifted her hand to show him, but, in fact, her whole body was trembling. "A bit of a shock."

He came to stand beside her. "Sue's still here. She's in her office. I'll ask if she's got a drop of brandy."

Sue came out with some water. Lydia sipped it in silence, Sue and Desmond hovering over her with concern.

"Did you know him well?" Sue asked after a while.

"A bit. We discussed things. We went to the choir together."

"Kept himself to himself," Sue said.

Lydia wanted to ask what he looked like, did he look peaceful, but suspected Sue would reply with bland words, well-rehearsed not to upset people.

The best thing to do was to stay in the flat and ponder the death of Clive, dwell on it, face it. That way, like Rosie's advice on the occasion she'd first met her that wet day in January, she would come to accept it. Never mind what people thought. Sit and think, contemplate the great mystery of death, that was what she needed to do. Clive would be proud of her.

After the second day, she ventured out. She needed to make a foray into the supermarket for food. Down the corridor she saw that the door of Clive's flat was open. That was disturbing. She walked along to investigate. A man appeared in the doorway.

"You couldn't tell me where to take rubbish, could you?" he said.

"Yes. There. Next to the lift. It's a rubbish chute." She paused to take a deep breath. "I'm really sorry about Clive." She looked at him. "Are you clearing his flat?"

He pitched a bag of rubbish down the chute.

"Yes, at this stage, I'm looking for documents. Insurance and stuff. I'm his brother, Charles, Charles Morris."

"Lydia Grover. We were friends, Clive and I. I thought he didn't have any family," she said crossly, "none that he was in touch with, anyway." She gazed at him. He did have a resemblance to Clive.

"That's right. I haven't been in touch. It was one of those family things. I meant to, but I left it too late."

"We were both in the choir." She was indignant, she wanted to claim Clive. This man had neglected him. She could see he didn't believe her. "I knew about his sexual orientation." That was the phrase Clive had taught her to use.

He relaxed. "Oh, yes. That has been an issue in the family. Why don't you come in, I can explain then."

He left the front door open as he led her into the sitting-room. She had never been in Clive's flat. Charles Morris had papers spread out on a small table. She sat on a chair in the window. The flat was furnished sparsely but was tidy.

"I haven't been here long, a few months. Clive was so helpful. I shall miss him terribly."

"If you were in the choir, you'd know what music he'd have wanted for the funeral."

"Of course. Some of the choir will come and sing if I ask. He liked 'In Paradisum', from Faure's Requiem. I'm glad he's got family after all."

"It was his lifestyle that caused the rift. I didn't understand until recently. It was a family stance. You don't deviate from a position like that in the sort of family we are. At least, I understand a bit more now. My grandson told me he's gay and as I'm fond enough of my one and only grandson, I had to get to grips with it, family or no. Poor old Clive, what a life he had. And ended so abruptly."

"I think he was well prepared." She wanted to comfort him now, comfort him about Clive and about his grandson. She gazed at him. "But you know, there's a lot of it about, isn't there? My own daughter recently told me, at thirty-six, that she is gay." She found her face lifting into a smile, the first for a couple of days. "I've never been in his flat before. He was a very private person." Her voice wavered now.

"I'm gratified that someone's mourning his departure. I haven't seen him for many, many, years. Just one call from his solicitor I had. Quite a shock. Look, I'd offer you a drink but I can't find any here."

"He didn't touch it. He was alcoholic."

It was his turn to gaze. "That, too? Poor Clive. Wish I'd known, I wish I'd understood." He sighed and pushed away some of the papers. "Tell me about him."

"He was a very sorted, self-sufficient person. He depended on no one but himself, but was caring, compassionate. He helped me a lot. When will the funeral be? I intend to come. I know he wanted to be buried, not cremated."

"You know a lot about him. Which flat is yours? I can let you know when I hear."

"I'm number twenty-nine. I won't keep you. I'm on my way out, really."

* * *

Walking to the supermarket, she had a spring in step. Her instinct was to curb it until she reflected that Clive would not mind. In fact, he would have been as pleased as she was that she had been able to talk about him, celebrate him, even. He had lived, and lived thoroughly, completely.

She finished her shopping to return to the flat, her head still full of Clive. Even the doubt that, as Sue had claimed, he did not suffer, was discarded with the acceptance that if he did, it had not been for long.

She'd not been back many minutes when her doorbell rang, followed by an informal tap on the door. She peered through the spy-hole. It was Charles Morris. He must have watched for her return.

"Lydia," he said as she opened the door, "I was looking for a keepsake, something of Clive's for you. This is the best I could do. It's silk." He held out a scarf of muted and fused shades of mauves, purples and blues.

With blurry eyes, she stared at the scarf he held out in his hands. The moment was both sad and beautiful. "How lovely! I shall cherish this forever. Thank you so much. Such a kind thought." She raised a smiling face. "I really am pleased."

"It's a man's scarf –," he began.

"It's mine now," she said, touching it to her cheek.

"I have his rings but I thought they'd be too large for you and too heavy. I can give them to my grandson, a token of, a symbol even, of my acceptance of his life."

He left, with a promise to let her know when the funeral would be. She undertook to arrange the music with the choir.

* * *

Charles Morris called at her flat a few times with details about the undertakers', the funeral service and the burial in the local cemetery. She made a visit to the undertakers' and planted a kiss on a stone cold forehead and left. Clive's funeral was held in the church round the corner from Tarascon Court on a sunny May afternoon.

"I want you to sit at the front of the church," Charles told her, "with me and Luke, my grandson."

"I think there'll be a few people from Tarascon Court," she said, "and quite a few members of the choir want to come. We won't be the only people there, though I know Clive was convinced no one would turn up."

"How did you come to be talking about such things?"

"We attended a series of talks about ageing and the taboos around it. He was very upfront about such things. I told you, he was sorted."

She wore a black dress with Clive's silk scarf loosely around her neck. About twenty people were in the church, most of them from the choir. The service was incongruously grim on such a brilliant day, even *In Paradisum'* not sounding to her as it usually did. Charles asked her to accompany him and his grandson in the car immediately behind the hearse on the way to the cemetery. She saw another car following them. Once around the grave, the occupants were revealed to be other members of the family who stood back from Charles, Luke and Lydia, their hostile glances showing their disapproval of Clive and, it seemed, Charles, and his grandson, Luke, also, a good-looking young man in his mid-twenties. Five wreaths were heaped by the grave side. Lydia could not help making a comparison with the mountain of flowers that had cascaded over Veronica's coffin.

Afterwards, Charles took her, with Luke, to the Castle Hotel for dinner.

* * *

A few weeks before the wedding, Ellie and Rosie visited Lydia at her flat to hand her an invitation.

Lydia read aloud, "An invitation to attend the marriage of Eleanor Rose, daughter of Lydia Grover and the late Michael Furlong and Rosemary Anne, daughter of Maria and Thomas Power to be celebrated at the Friends' Meeting House, Sittendon, and after wards at the Castle Hotel…"

Lydia looked up at the proud couple and smiled. This had not been her dream for her daughter but then it was not her life. And Ellie had recovered her glow.

"My parents are coming," Rosie said. "I'm so relieved. It wouldn't have been the same without them."

They all sat down and Lydia poured each a glass of wine to celebrate.

"I've decided to give up making meringues," Ellie said. "It's so farcical all that elaborate expense for one day. I can't support it any longer. But meringues have helped me to save up a decent sum for our future."

From Lydia, there would be a sizeable wedding present for the couple. She was able to help both her daughters in the ways they needed and that was most pleasing to her, even though Ellie's share would end up in Australia. She recalled the bus trip on that wet evening, her first encounter with Rosie and the first intimation that her own life must change. It had been less than six months ago.

"I think my Dad will lend or give me something," Rosie was saying, "towards my studio. So we are both set up for the future."

"In Australia," Lydia could not help herself.

"No," Ellie said casually, but with a mischievous grin, "not Australia. We've changed our minds. We couldn't go that far, neither of us has the guts. No, we're moving up North."

* * *

Preparations for the wedding were a huge secret but facts slipped out.

185

"We're not being bridesmaids," Polly told Lydia on a visit with Jez, "we are being attendants." She sounded disappointed.

"Sounds like much the same thing," Lydia said.

"And neither Ellie nor Rosie will be given away. Rosie says she belongs to herself not to anyone else, not even Ellie, either before or after the wedding."

"And what will you be wearing?" Lydia said.

"I'm not allowed to tell," said Polly.

"She won't tell me, either," said Jez.

"And I'm not allowed to say what Ellie and Rosie are wearing except that it's identical and I've seen them."

Lydia hoped neither Ellie nor Rosie was to be dressed as a man. If the outfits were identical surely that ruled that out? Or did it? She'd had no experience of a same-sex wedding. Her concern was kept to herself.

For her own outfit for the wedding, she chose a dress in powder blue, loose enough to disguise her lumps and bumps, and found a fascinator in a matching colour. Clive's scarf was added. It was to be a midsummer wedding, giving a long, light evening for celebration and partying.

When she awoke, on the morning, to the tree-tops chorus of birds, a blue sky promised a beautiful day. From her bedroom window she watched the sun rising higher. The year was halfway through. Six months had passed since Christmas and there was another six months before the next one, by which time she would be seventy. That felt like a watershed. After seventy, it was downhill all the way. Or was it? Habitual thinking was now challenged by habitual questioning. Much had happened since Christmas, Kate's marriage was over, Ellie was about to marry a woman, Nick had all but left home, Polly was well-embedded (surely that was the appropriate word?) with Jez and she herself had a new home, new friends, as well as new interests, some of which she had modified lately. Too much of a good thing could be exhausting. Life was good, serene now and fulfilling. She regretted nothing.

Ellie and Rosie arrived together at the Meeting House. Sitting in the front row, Lydia was aware of the frisson rippling through the assembled families and friends. She turned her head and there they were, in the doorway, in matching cream outfits, soft tunics and flowing trousers, carrying identical posies of pink roses with a pink rose each in their hair. Lydia wanted to cry already. She felt in her handbag for a tissue.

Ellie was radiant. That was her daughter, Lydia told herself, making this courageous statement. Happiness shone from the couple. Polly and Lily, Rosie's sister, were in pink versions of Ellie's and Rosie's outfits, carrying posies of cream roses, with cream roses in their hair. Jez, sitting on the end of the row, reached out to Polly, as she passed. Polly, looking stunning, mimed him a kiss.

"Eleanor Rose will you take Rosemary Anne... and commit to a loving and caring partnership?"

How beautiful it sounded, despite the difference from the conventional fairytale magic. How real, how serious too, was the impact the proceedings made. Lydia, as Ellie's mother, and Rosie's father were the witnesses. Lydia had a shock as she went forward to perform this legal requirement. Rosie's father, the up-to-now disapproving parent, was white, another prejudice, another assumption to be examined. Lydia's shame would have overwhelmed her once, to mar her pride in the whole occasion, a celebration involving the bridging of many gaps, but on this occasion, it was just another of life's lessons.

"You look stunning, Mum." Kate wandered over during the photograph session. "Love your outfit. You'll be next."

"To do what?"

"Get married, of course."

"No, Kate. You will. Why on earth would I get married again? All that adapting, adjusting. I'm too old to have children. I'm totally happy in my little flat."

"That's an awful lot of reasons, Mum."

"How are you?" Lydia parried. "You look lovely." Kate was wearing a shimmering deep blue outfit.

Kate's eyes filled, unexpectedly. "I never imagined it would be so painful, splitting up."

"I see." Lydia was careful. She was tempted to point out that her defection to Peter had been viewed as sailing off into the sunset to a life of bliss. It had been nothing of the sort, especially with Kate's and Ellie's efforts to ruin it all.

"I want it, though. Thanks, Mum, for everything."

Lydia gave her a hug, said nothing.

"But I'm coping. It's too soon to find someone else. But I'm content, let's leave it at that. Me and Polly, in the house, we're fine. With the occasional royal visit from Nick. I'll see you, Mum."

Kate slipped away.

For the wedding breakfast, Lydia was seated next to a male relative of Rosie's. Further long the table, Polly was making meaningful gestures and expressions in her direction, rolling her eyes and grinning. She sought out Lydia later, several drinks later.

"We saw you, me and Jez, sitting next to Rosie's uncle. You'll be next."

"Next for what, Polly?"

"To get married, of course."

"What's the matter with everyone, trying to get me married off again? I had a similar conversation with Kate earlier. I have no intention of marrying again."

"But you'll be lonely."

"No, I won't."

A knowing expression crept over Polly's face. "I know. You're just going to have it off with someone, aren't you, like you said once."

"Polly, I think you've had far too much to drink. I never said anything of the sort."

"Yes, you did. You implied it. It comes to the same thing. You are a very saucy grandmother." She wagged her finger at Lydia. "I shall tell Jez."

Dancing was about to begin. The floor was cleared and the band struck up. Ellie and Rosie went to the centre of the floor. They danced a rumba, a dance of love, instead of the traditional smoochy waltz.

And what a dance it was. With each gazing into the eyes of the other, the performance had an intensity that was powerful and erotic, something that Lydia had not before perceived or understood between the two women. So careful had they been not to shock or embarrass others, she realised, and now they were approved of legally and socially and could allow their emotions to be displayed in public as any opposite sex couple would have done at this point. Lydia found the dance disturbing, exciting, passionate. When it ended, Ellie and Rosie clung to each other for several moments. A stunned silence followed, then applause broke out.

Lydia understood, now. This was not friendship alone but much, much more. There was a depth in their feelings for each other that she had not appreciated. With sadness, she recalled young Gary Grover, who had had this ability and opportunity to love passionately, severely curtailed and denied. No wonder Ellie had been hurt.

After a while, Lydia rose, bade farewell quietly to Ellie and Rosie, and slipped out. A darkening sky, a setting sun, greeted her. A car slid up to the pavement outside the hotel. The door opened to allow her to slip in. Her attention was caught by a movement at the doorway. She had a moment earlier come through it. Polly was checking up on her.

THE END

Acknowledgements

Thanks to Matt Maguire of Candescent Press
for the cover and for technical support.

To Pete Currie, Sylvia Daly for their support.

Also by Maggie Redding

ALMOST PARADISE
(Book 1 of the Faradise Series)

NOTHING LIKE PARADISE
(Book 2 of the Faradise Series)

and – coming soon –

IT SOUNDS LIKE PARADISE
(Book 3 of the Faradise Series)

HOLD FAST TO DREAMS

A LIFE WORTH LOVING

COMMON GROUND

THE EDUCATION OF MATTIE DOBSON

**For further information please see my website
www.maggieredding.com**

48352107R00112

Printed in Poland
by Amazon Fulfillment
Poland Sp. z o.o., Wrocław